A BOOK OF

# Phrases

—A PERFECT REFERENCE COMPANION



**Josef S. Verghese**

**BEST FOR STUDENTS, TEACHERS & LEARNERS OF ENGLISH LANGUAGE**

MG BOOKS

NEW DELHI (INDIA)

# PHRASES



*Published by*

MG BOOKS

*An Imprint of*

MAANU GRAPHICS

**MAANU GRAPHICS**
**(PUBLISHERS OF GENERAL BOOKS)**
5FF, Ganpati Bhawan, 21 Ansari Road,
Darya Ganj, New Delhi-110002
Ph: 65285220, 64138266
E-mail : maanugraphics@yahoo.com
mgbooks.maanu@yahoo.com



*Printed at*
Satyam Enterprises, Delhi

# CONTENTS

# A

ABANDON

— **abandon somebody/something to somebody/ something** to go away from a person, thing or place not intending to return.

ABOUT

— **about time**-used to express the idea that something should have already happened

— **out and about**-resorted to normal activity.

— **to hang about**- to wait or stay near a place with or without a particular aim or purpose

— **to come about**-to take place

— **to bring about**- to cause to happen

ABHOR

— **to have abhorrence of**- to detest, to have extreme hatred for.

ABOVE

— **above board** open, honest and without trickery.

— **above (someone's) head** too difficult to understand.

— **above suspicion** too much respected or thought to be too honourable to be suspected of doing wrong.

— **get a bit above oneself** to become very vain or conceited.

ABSENT

— **absent minded** inattentive.

ABSTRACT

— **to abstract a thing from** to withdraw, to take out.

ABUNDANCE

— **in abundance** in great quantity, in plenty, more

than needed.

ACCEDE
— **accede to** accept.

ACCESS
— **access to** approach to.

ACCENT
— **to put accent on** to stress, to emphasize.

ACCIDENT
— **accidents will happen** things go wrong at some time in everyone's life.
— **a chapter of accidents** a series of misfortunes.

ACCOMPANY
— **accompany with** to support, to keep company with.

ACCORD
— **according to one's lights** in keeping with one's beliefs or attitudes.
— **of one's own accord** of one's own free will, without being forced.
— **with one accord** together, in unison.

ACCORDANCE
— **in accordance with** in a manner consistent with.

ACCORDING
— **according to** in conformity with.

ACCOUNT
— **by all accounts** in the opinion of most people.
— **give a good account of oneself** to do well.
— **on my** *or* **your** *or* **his** *or* **her, etc, account** because of me, etc, for my, etc, sake.
— **on no account** not for any reason whatsoever.

ACCUSE
— **accuse of** to bring a charge against.
— **accuse for** to charge for committing a crime.

ACCUSTOM
— **accustom of** to make familiar by custom, to become habitat, to habituate.

ACHILLES
— **Achilles' heel** the one weak spot in a person.

ACID
— **acid test** a test that will prove or disprove something conclusively.

ACQUIT
— **acquit oneself of** to declare innocent, to discharge.
— **to acquit well** to behave nicely, to fare nicely.

ACROSS
— **across the board** applying to everyone or to all cases.
— **put one across on (someone)** to deceive or trick (someone).

ACTION
— **action stations** a state of preparedness for some activity.
— **get a piece** *or* **slice of the action** to be involved in something, get a share of something.

AD
— **ad hoc** for a particular (usually exclusive) purpose.
— **ad infinitum** without limit or end.
— **ad-lib** to speak without preparation, to improvise.

ADD
— **add fuel to the fire** to make a difficult situation worse.
— **add insult to injury** to make matters worse.

ADDRESS
— **address to** speak or write to.
— **address oneself to** to set about, to do a particular task.

ADVANTAGE

— **have the advantage of (someone)** to recognize (someone) without oneself being recognized by that person.
— **take advantage of (someone)** to exploit or make use of (someone) for one's own ends.
— **take advantage of (something)** to make use of (something), to put (something) to good use.
— **to advantage** favourably, so that the good points are emphasized.

AFIELD

— **Far afield** at a distance.
— **Ad-Interim** for the meantime, serving for a limited period, present interval.

AFTER

— **after a fashion** in a manner that is barely adequate.
— **aftermath** something that happens after, or as a result of, an important, often a disastrous, event.
— **after (someone's) own heart** to one's liking; liked or admired by (someone).
— **after the fact** after something, especially a crime, has taken place.

AGAIN

— **again and again** repeatedly.
— **time and again** many a time; often.

AGAINST

— **against the clock** in a hurry to get something done before a certain time.
— **be up against it** to be in a difficult or dangerous situation.

AGE

— **a golden age** a time of great achievement.
— **a ripe old age** a very old age.
— **of a certain age** no longer young.
— **come of age** to reach the age when one is legally considered an adult (in Britain 18).
— **the age of consent** the age someone must be before

he or she can legally have sexual intercourse.
— **under age** under the legal age for something, too young.

AGENDA
— **a hidden agenda** things which someone secretly wants to achieve from a situation while pretending to have another goal.

AGONY
— **agony aunt** *or* **uncle** a woman or man who gives advice on personal problems either in a newspaper or magazine column, or on television or radio.
— **agony column** a newspaper or magazine column in which readers write in with their problems, which are answered by the agony aunt or uncle.

AHEAD
— **ahead of the game** in an advantageous position; in front of one's rivals.
— **ahead of time** early, before the appointed time.
— **streets ahead of (someone** *or* **something)** much better than (someone or something).

AID
— **aid and abet (someone)** to help and encourage (someone), especially in something wrong or illegal.
— **what is (something) in aid of?** what is (something) for? Why has (something) been done?.

AIM
— **aim at** to point at with a weapon, to set oneself to.
— **to set aim at** to desire and work for.

AIR
— **air** *or* **wash one's dirty linen in public** to discuss private or personal matters in public.
— **air** one's grievances to make public one's complaints.
— **clear the air** to make a situation less tense.
— **hot air** boasting; empty or meaningless words.
— **in the air** current; around; in circulation.
— **on the air** on radio or television.

— **put on airs** to behave as though one were superior to others, to act in a conceited way.
— **take the air** go for a walk or a drive.
— **up in the air** uncertain, undecided.
— **walk on air** to be very happy.

ALL
— **all and sundry** everybody, one and all.
— **all chiefs and no Indians** a surplus of people wishing to give orders or to administrate and a deficiency of people willing to carry orders out or to do the work.
— **all** ears listening intently.
— **all for (someone *or* something)** completely in favour of (someone or something).
— **all hours** for long periods of time, from early in the morning until late at night.
— **all in** exhausted.
— **all in all** taking everything into consideration.
— **all in one piece** safely, undamaged.
— **all out** with as much effort as possible.
— **all over** at an end.
— **all over bar the shouting** at an end to all intents and purposes.
— **all set** ready to go, prepared.
— **all-singing, all-dancing** of a machine, system, very advanced with a great many modern features, sometimes not all necessary.
— **all the best** best wishes, good luck.
— **all there** having all one's faculties, alert and intelligent.
— **all told** altogether, including everything or everyone.
— **be all things to all men** to try constantly to agree with or fit in with whomever one is with at the time.
— **it is all up with (someone)** there is no hope left for (someone).
— **on all fours** on one's hands and knees.

ALLEY
— **alley cat** a wild or promiscuous person.

— **blind alley** an action or situation that cannot be advantageous.

ALLIANCE

— **an unholy alliance** used of an association or partnership between two people or organizations that have nothing in common and would not normally work together, especially when this association has a bad purpose.

ALLOWANCE

— **make allowances for (someone)** to expect a less high standard from (someone) because of particular circumstances.

ALMA MATER

— one's old university, college or school.

ALONE

— **all alone** single handed.

— **go it alone** do a task without anyone's help.

— **let alone** without considering.

ALONG

— **Along with** in the company of.

— **All along** throughout.

— **Along for the ride (informal)** not taking any active part.

— **Alpha and Omega** The beginning and the end.

ALPHA

— **alpha and omega** the beginning and the end.

ALSO

— **also-ran** an unsuccessful person.

ALTERNATIVE

— **alternative medicine** the treatment of diseases or disorders that uses techniques other than those of conventional medicine, including homoeopathy, osteopathy, acupuncture, aromatherapy, etc.

— **have no alternative** to be forced to take a certain course of action because it is the only possible one.

ALTOGETHER
— **in the altogether** in the nude.

AMAZE
— **amazed at** confounded.
— **amazed with** surprised.

AMAZON
— a very strong or well-built woman.

AMEND
— **to make amend** to compensate, to fill the gap.

AMERICAN
— **as American as apple pie** typical of the traditional American way of life or culture.
— **the American dream** the hope of achieving success and prosperity through hard work, from the dreams which immigrants had when they landed in America to start a new life.

AMISS
— **take (something) amiss** to take offence or be upset at (something).

AND
— **And no mistake (informal)** and more as well (used for emphasis).
— **And then some (informal)** and more as well (used for emphasis)

ANGEL
— **an angel of mercy** a person who gives help and comfort, especially one who appears unexpectedly.
— **angels' visits** visits that are rare and short but very pleasant.
— **a fallen angel** a person who had formerly a good reputation for being virtuous or successful but no longer does so.
— **entertain an angel unawares** to meet and talk to someone whose worth or fame one is unaware of.
— **on the side of the angels** supporting or agreeing

with what is regarded as being the good or the right side.

— **write like an angel** to write well and movingly.

ANVIL

— **anvil on or upon the anvil** under discussion, on the agenda.

ANY

— **anybody's guess** something which no one can be certain about.

— **any day** whatever the circumstances.

— **any old how** in an untidy and careless way.

— **anything but** not at all.

— **anything goes** any kind of behaviour, dress, etc, is acceptable.

— **like anything** very much, hard, fast, energetically, etc.

ANYTHING

— **anything but** definitely not.

— **anything like** in any way similar.

APACE

— **to keep apace** to move with.

APARTHY

— **to show an apathy** to be indifferent.

APART

— **be poles** *or* **worlds apart** to be completely different.

— **take (someone) apart** to scold or criticize (someone) severely.

APE

— **go ape** to become extremely angry or excited.

APEX

— **To be on the apex** to be at the highest point

APOLOGY

— **an apology for (something)** a very poor example of

(something).

APOSTLE

— **Apostle of peace** one who preaches peace.
— **Apostle of** advocate of

APPEAR

— **to put up an appearance** to appear in person.

APPEARANCE

— **keep up appearances** to behave in public in such a way as to hide what is going on in private.
— put in an appearance at (something) to attend a meeting, function, etc, especially for a short time or because it is one's duty to do so.

APPETITE

— **to whelm appetite** to create a desire for food.

APPLE

— **apple of discord** a cause of quarrelling.
— **apple-pie bed** a bed made up, as a practical joke, in such a way that it is impossible to get into.
— **in apple-pie order** with everything tidy and correctly arranged.
— **apples and oranges** two things which are completely different and so should not be compared.
— **rotten apple** a person who is bad or unsatisfactory and will have a bad influence on others.
— **the apple of (someone's) eye** a favourite, a person who is greatly loved by (someone).
— **upset the apple-cart** to spoil plans or arrangements.

APPLY

— **apply to** to make a request to a person, to request for a particular thing.
— **to apply oneself to** to devote..

APPOINT

— **appoint to** to assign, to name to an office.

APRON
— **tied to (someone's) apron-strings** completely dependent on a woman, especially one's mother or wife.

ARAB
— **A Street Arab** an uncared child in a large city

ARGUE
— **To argue with about/over** exchange angry words
— **To argue into** to persuade a person to take to a certain course.
— **To argue out** of-to persuade a person not to take a certain course

ARGUMENT
— **To have an argument with** to have a heated discussion with a person; a quarrel

ARK
— **like something out of the ark** very old-fashioned looking.

ARM
— **armed to the hilt** *or* **teeth** provided with all the equipment that one could possibly need.
— **be up in arms** to protest angrily.
— **chance one's arm** to take a risk.
— **cost an arm and a leg** to cost a great deal of money.
— **give one's right arm for (something)** to be willing to go to any lengths to get something.
— **keep (someone) at arm's length** to avoid becoming too close to or too friendly with someone.
— **lay down one's arms** to stop fighting or opposing.
— **the long arm of the law** the power or authority of the police.
— **put the arm on (someone)** to try to force someone to do what you want.
— **right arm** chief source of help and support.
— **take up arms** to become actively involved in a quarrel or dispute.
— **twist (someone's) arm** to force (someone) to do

(something), to persuade (someone) to do (something).
— **with one arm tied behind one's back** very easily.
— **with open arms** welcomingly.

ARMOUR
— **chink in (someone's) armour** a weak or vulnerable spot in someone who is otherwise very strong and difficult to get through to or attack.
— **knight in shining armour** a person who it is hoped will save a situation or come to one's aid.

AROUND
— **have been around** (1) to have had a lot of experience of life.
(2) to have been alive.

ARRIVE
— **arrive at** to reach any place, situation, or decision.

ARROW
— **a straight arrow** a person who is completely honest, moral and trustworthy.

ARTHUR
— **not to know if one is Arthur or Martha** to be very confused because one has too much to do.

ARTICLE
— **the genuine article** used to emphasize that something is real and not a copy.

AS
— **as a rule** normally, usually.
— **As good as almost** nearly.
— **as it were** used in making comparisons.
— **as of** from a certain date.
— **as to** with regard to; on the matter of.

ASHES
— **rake over the ashes** to discuss things that are passed, especially things that are best forgotten.
— **rise from the ashes** to develop and flourish out of

ruin and destruction.

— **the Ashes** the trophy, originally mythical, contended for in the cricket test matches between Britain and Australia.

ASK

— **be asking for it** to behave in such a way as to invite something unpleasant, such as a beating.

— **be (someone's) for the asking** for something to be available to someone who wishes it without payment.

ASPIRE

— **Aspire to** to aim at.

— **Aspire for** desire for achievement of (something).

ASSAULT

— **to make an assault** to attack suddenly, to attack beyond expectation.

AT

— **At a blow** single stroke/one stroke quickly, with one action.

— **At all costs** without fail, no matter what sacrifice has to be made.

— **At a loose end** with nothing to do.

— **At any rate** nevertheless; at least.

— **At one's heels** very close, near (with reference to a person who is being followed or pursued).

— **At issue** in dispute.

— **At one's wits' end** in a state where one does not know what to do.

— **At (the) worst** according to the worst result that one can imagine.

— **At a law ebb** decline.

— **At a stretch** without a break.

— **At one' beck and call** always at one's service or command..

— **At a standstill** without any further movement.

ATONE

— **Atone for** to make up for deficiencies.

ATTACK

— **Blunt the attack** reduce its effect.

ATTEND

— **To attend upon** to wait upon, to keep attention.

ATTENDANCE

— **dance attendance on (someone)** to stay close to (someone) in order to carry out all his or her wishes and so gain favour.

— **auld lang syne** times that are past, especially times remembered with fondness.

AUNT

— **Aunt Sally** a person or thing that is being subjected to general abuse, mockery and criticism.

AVAIL

— **of no avail** of no use, without effect.

— **to no avail** without success.

AVENUE

— **explore every avenue** make a thorough enquiry.

AVERSE

— **averse to** having dislike for, having hatred for.

AVERSON

— **averse to** having dislike for, having hatred for.

AWAKE

— **awake to something** become aware of.

AWAY

— **do away with (someone *or* something)** to get rid of something, to abolish something.

— **get away from it all** to escape from the problems of daily life, usually by taking a holiday.

— **get away with you!** I don't believe you!

— **the one that got away** a chance of success which one either did not or could not take of advantage at the time but which one always remembers.

# B

BABE

— **babe in arms** an inexperienced or naive person.

— **babes in the wood** people who are naive, inexperienced and too trusting.

BABY

— **be (someone's) baby** to be the responsibility or special interest of someone.

— **be left holding the baby** to be left to cope with a difficult situation that has been abandoned by the person who is really responsible for it.

— **throw out the baby with the bath water** accidentally to get rid of something desirable or essential when trying to get rid of undesirable or unnecessary things.

— **wet the baby's head** to have a drink to celebrate the birth of a baby.

BACK

— **back number** a person or thing that is no longer of importance or of use.

— **back scratching** doing favours for someone so that he or she will in turn do favours for one.

— **back to the drawing board** it will be necessary to start again on a project or activity.

— **back to the grindstone** back to work.

— **backwater** an isolated place unaffected by what is happening in the world outside.

— **break one's back** to put in a great deal of effort.

— **break the back of (something)** to complete the largest or most difficult part.

— **get off (someone's) back** to stop harassing or bothering (someone).

— **have come a long way** to have changed or improved a great deal since starting out.

— **have (someone *or* something) at one's back** have (someone or something) as a help or support.
— **have one's back to the wall.** to be in a very difficult or desperate situation.
— **have a broad back** to be able to deal with a great deal of responsibility or with a great many problems.
— **know (something) backwards *or* like the back of one's hand** to know all there is to know about (something).
— **know (someone *or* something) like the back of one's hand** to know (someone or something) very well indeed.

BAD
— **bad egg** a worthless or law-breaking person.
— **badly off** without much money.
— **go to the bad** to become immoral or criminal.
— **have it bad/have got it bad** to be very much in love with someone.
— **hit a bad patch** to encounter difficulties or a difficult period.
— **in bad odour** in disfavour.
— **in (someone's) bad *or* black books** out of favour with (someone).
— **not half bad** quite good, very good.
— **too bad** unfortunate.
— **with a bad grace** in an unwilling and bad-tempered way.

BAG
— **bag and baggage** all one's belongings, or equipment.
— **bag lady** a homeless woman who carries all her belongings with her in bags.
— **bag of bones** a person who is extremely thin.

— **bag** of **nerves** a very nervous or anxious person.
— **bag of tricks** the equipment necessary to do something.
— **cannot punch one's way out of a paper bag** to be totally lacking in ability or power.
— **in the bag** certain to be obtained.
— **mixed bag** a very varied mixture.

— **pack one's bags** to leave somewhere, sometimes suddenly.

BALANCE
— in the balance undecided, uncertain.
— **on balance** considering everything.
— **strike a balance** to reach an acceptable compromise.
— **throw (someone) off balance** to cause (someone) to be disconcerted or confused.
— **tip the balance** to exert an influence which, although slight, is enough to alter the outcome of something.

BALD
— **bald as a coot** extremely bald.

BALL[1]
— **have a ball** to have a very enjoyable time.

BALL[2]
— **a ball and chain** someone or something that restricts your freedom to do what you want.
— **a whole new ball game** used to emphasize how much a situation has changed.
— **be in the right ballpark** to be reasonably close to the amount which is required or wanted.
— **drop the ball** to make a mistake or fail to do something.
— **have the ball at one's feet** to be in a position to be successful.
— **on the ball** alert, quick-witted, attentive to what is going on around one.
— **pick up/take the ball and run with it** to take an idea, project, etc, which someone else has started and try to make it successful.
— **play ball** to act in accordance with someone else's wishes.
— **play ball with (someone)** to cooperate with (someone).
— **set** *or* **start the ball rolling** to start off an activity of some kind, often a discussion.
— **the whole ball of wax** *(especially American English)*

used to emphasize that you are referring to absolutely all of something.

BALLISTIC
— **go ballistic** suddenly to become extremely angry.

BALLOON
— **go down like a lead balloon** of a suggestion, idea, joke, etc., to be very badly received.
— **when the balloon goes up** when something serious, usually something that is expected and feared, happens.

BANANA
— **go bananas** to go mad, to get extremely angry.
— **slip on a banana skin** to do something that causes one humiliation or public embarrassment.

BAND
— **a one-man band** an organization which is run by one person only.
— **jump on the bandwagon** to show an interest in, or become involved in, something simply because it is fashionable or financially advantageous.
— **looking** as **though one has stepped out of a bandbox** looking very neat and elegant.

BANDWAGON
— **Jump on the bandwagon** join others in doing something fashionable

BANE
— **The bane of one's existence/life** cause of one's ruin.
— **Go off with a bang** be very successful.
— **Bang goes something** lost, something is suddenly gone.

BANNER
— **Under the banner** claiming a support

BANG
— **bang goes (something)** that puts a sudden end to

(something).
— **bang one's head against a brick wall** to do (something) in vain.
— **bang on** exactly, precisely.
— **go with a bang** to be very successful.

BANK
— **break the bank** to leave (oneself or someone) without any money.

BAPTISM
— **baptism of fire** a first, usually difficult or unpleasant, experience of something.

BAR
— **behind bars** in prison.

BARE
— **bare one's soul** to tell (someone) one's private feelings or thoughts.
— **the bare bones of (something)** the essential and basic details of (something).
— **with one's bare hands** using one's hands rather than tools or weapons.

BARGAIN
— **get more than one bargained for** to encounter more difficulty than one had expected or was prepared for.
— **into the bargain** in addition, as well.
— **drive a hard bargain** to try to get a deal that is very favourable to oneself.
— **strike a bargain** to reach a settlement or agreement.

BARGE
— **wouldn't touch (someone *or* something) with a bargepole.** to wish to have absolutely no contact with (someone or something).

BARK
— **bark up the wrong tree** to have the wrong idea or impression about (something), to approach

(something) in the wrong way.

— **(someone's) bark is worse than his *or* her bite** a person is not as dangerous or as harmful as he or she appears to be.

BARREL

— **have (someone) over a barrel** to get (someone) into such a position that one can get him or her to do anything that one wants.

— **scrape the (bottom of the) barrel** to have to use someone or something of poor or inferior quality because that is all that is available.

— **with both barrels** forcefully and fiercely.

BASE

— **get to *or* make *or* reach first base** to complete the important first stage of a process.

— **touch base with (someone)** to be in contact with (someone), to talk to someone.

BAT[1]

— **go to bat for (someone)** to offer someone help or support

— **off one's own bat** by oneself, without the help or permission of any one else.

— **play a straight bat** to act in an honest and fair way.

BAT[2]

— **blind as a bat** having very poor eyesight.

— **like a bat out of hell** very quickly.

BATE

— **with bated breath** anxiously.

BATH

— **blood bath** killing of many people on one occasion.

BATTERY

— **to change one's battery** to alter the direction of attack.

BATTLE

— **be half the battle** used to indicate an important or difficult or part of something is over and that the rest will be easier.

— **the battle lines are drawn** used to indicate that two sides which are opposed to each other for some reason are ready to begin the fight, argument, competition, etc. and that their aims have been declared and made clear.

— **fight a losing battle** to keep trying to achieve something, although with no chance of success.

— **a running battle** an argument or fight which has lasted for a long time.

— **win the battle, but lose the war** to get some of the things which you wanted from an argument, discussion, etc. but to lose your most important goal.

BAY

— **keep (someone *or* something) at bay** to keep (someone or something) from coming too close.

BE

— **the be-all and end-all** the most important aim or purpose.

— **Be a devil (informal and humorous** be bold, brave

— **Be an angel** (informal) be kind, helpful

— **(not) Be one's day** (informal) (often with negative) (not) be lucky

— **To be in one's cup** under the spell of intoxication

— **To be in good books of** having a good impression

— **Be oneself** act naturally

BEAM

— **broad in the beam** wide in the hips or buttocks.

— **off beam** (1) on the wrong course.

(2) inaccurate.

— **on one's beam ends** very short of money.

BEAN

— **full of beans** very lively, in good spirits.

— **know how many beans make five** to be experienced in the ways of the world.

— **not have a bean** to have no money whatsoever.
— **not know beans about (something)** to know nothing whatsoever about (something).
— **not to amount to a hill of beans** to be of very little worth or significance.
— **not amount to a row of beans** *same as* **not amount to a hill of beans.**
— **spill the beans** to reveal a secret or confidential information.

BEAR[1]
— **bear down on (someone)** to come towards (someone) in a determined and often threatening way.
— **bear fruit** to produce results.
— **bear in mind** remember.
— **bear (something) out** to confirm (something).
— **bear up** to keep cheerful or strong under strain or stress.

BEAR[2]
— **bear garden** a noisy, rowdy place.
— **like a bear with a sore head** extremely bad-tempered.

BEARD
— **beard the lion in its den** to confront or face (someone) openly and boldly.

BEAT
— **beat about the bush** to approach (something) in an indirect way.
— **beat a (hasty) retreat** to run away.
— **beat (someone) hollow** to defeat (someone) soundly.
— **beat it** to run away.
— **beat the drum** to try to attract public attention.
— **beat (someone) to it** to succeed in doing something before someone else can.
— **if you can't beat them** *or* **'em, join them** *or* **'em** if you cannot persuade other people to think and act like you, the most sensible course of action is for you to begin to think and act like them.
— **off the beaten track** in an isolated position, away

from towns or cities.

— **take some** *or* **a lot of beating** to be of such high quality that it is difficult to improve on.

— **to beat the band** with great force or vigour.

— **without missing a beat** without hesitating or reacting to something surprising, unexpectedly difficult, etc.

BEAUTY

— **beauty is in the eye of the beholder** different people have different ideas of what is beautiful.

— **beauty is only skin deep** people have more important qualities than how they look. *Beauty is only skin deep.*

BEAVER

— **eager beaver** a very enthusiastic and hard-working person.

— **work like a beaver** to work very industriously and enthusiastically.

BECOME

— **what becomes of** what is happening to.

— **become of** to come to be.

BECK

— **at (someone's) beck and call** having to be always available to carry out (someone's) orders or wishes.

BED

— **bed of nails** *or* **thorns** a very unpleasant or difficult situation.

— **bed of roses** an easy, comfortable or happy situation.

— **get into bed with (someone)** to start working closely or cooperating with (someone).

— **get out of bed on the wrong side** to start the day in a very bad-tempered mood.

— **put (something) to bed** to complete (something), to finish dealing with (something).

BEE

— **have a bee in one's bonnet** to have an idea that one cannot stop thinking or talking about, to have an obsession.

— **busy bee** a person who is very active and industrious.
— **make a beeline for (someone *or* something)** to go directly and quickly to (someone or something).
— **think one *or* someone is the bee's knees** to consider oneself or someone else to very special and important.

BEEN

— **have been around** have a wide experience of life.
— **have been there before** know all about a situation because you have experienced it.

BEFORE

— **before one can say Jack Robinson** very rapidly, in an instant.
— **before one knows where one is** very quickly, before one can grasp the situation.
— **before the flood** a very long time ago.

BEG

— **beggar description** to be such that words cannot describe it.
— **beg the question** in an argument, to take for granted the very point that requires to be proved; to fail to deal effectively with the point being discussed.
— **going a-begging** unclaimed or unsold.

BEGGAR

— **Beggar description** be impossible to describe properly.
— **Beggars can't be choosers** when there is no choice, you have to be satisfied with whatever you can get.

BEGIN

— **To begin with** at first, at the time of starting.
— **Well begun is half done** a good start assures success.
— **Beginner's luck** good luck or success at the start of learning to do something.

BEHALF

— **In behalf of somebody** in order to help somebody.

— **On behalf of somebody** as the representative of somebody or instead of them.

BEHIND

— **Behind someone's back** secretly; without someone knowing.

— **Behind bars** in prison.

— **Behind closed doors** in secrecy.

— **Be behind something** be the reason for something.

— **Behind the scene** not in the open, in secret.

— **Put something behind one** think of something usually unpleasant as being in the past.

— **Fall behind** not keep up with.

BEHOLD

— **Behold to** obliged to.

BEING

— **Come into being** begin to exist.

BELIEF

— **Beyond belief** difficult to believe.

— **In the belief that** confident that.

— **To the best of my belief** as far as I know.

BELIEVE

— **Believe in** have faith in.

BELL

— **bell the cat** to be the person in a group who undertakes something dangerous for the good of the group.

— **ring a bell** to bring back vague memories.

— **saved by the bell** rescued from an unpleasant situation by something suddenly bringing that situation to an end.

BELLY

— **go belly-up** to fail, to go bankrupt.

— **have a bellyful of (something)** to have too much of (something) so that you are bored with it.

BELOW
— **Below one's dignity** below one's position.
— **Below the mark** not to the point, below the standard.
— **Below one's breath** silently.

BELT
— **below the belt** unfair.
— **belt and braces** used to describe extra precautions taken to make sure that all is well.
— **get/have (something) under one's belt** to have already done or achieved something worthwhile.
— **tighten one's belt** to reduce one's expenditure.
— **under one's belt** achieved or accomplished.

BERTH
— **give (someone) a wide berth** to keep well away from (someone).

BESIDE
— **be beside oneself** to be in a state of great emotion.
— **beside the point** not directly concerned with the issue being discussed.

BEST
— **do one's level best** to try as hard as one can.
— have the best of both worlds to benefit from the advantages of two sets of circumstances.
— **put one's best foot forward** to make the best attempt possible.
— **the best part of (something)** most of (something), nearly all of (something).
— **with the best of them** as well as other people who are more experienced, better qualified, etc.
— **with the best will in the world** no matter how much one wants to do something.

BET
— **all bets are off** used to indicate that it is impossible to predict what might happen in a particular situation.
— **hedge one's bets** to try to protect oneself from possible loss, failure, disappointment, etc.

BETE

— **Your, his etc., bete noire** a person or thing that particularly annoys you and that you do not like

BETTER

— **better off** (1) happier.

— **go one better than (someone)** to improve on something that someone has done.

— **get the better of (someone)** to overcome or defeat (some-one).

— **have seen better** days. to be no longer new or fresh.

— **the better part of (something)** a large part of (something), most of (something).

— **think better of (something)** to reconsider (something), to change one's mind about (something).

BEWARE

— **Beware of** be on guard, take care of.

BEYOND

— **Beyond belief** unbelievable, incredible.

— **Beyond measure (formal)** something that cannot be counted or measured.

— **Beyond the bounds** of outside.

— **(Put someone) beyond the pale** not acceptable in good or polite society.

— **Beyond one's comprehension** beyond one's power of understanding.

— **Beyond seas** abroad

BIAS

— **To be biased** one-sided inclination of mind, prejudiced.

— **Bid fair** look as if it (one) is going to (do something).

— **To bid fair** to promise well.

— **To bid farewell** to offer good wishes at the time of departing.

— **To bid defiance** to face challenge in life, to ignore.

— **To bid goodbye** to take leave at the time of departure.

BIDE

— **bide one's time** to wait for a suitable opportunity.

BIG

— **a big fish in a small pond** a person who seems better, more important, etc. than he or she is because he or she operates in a small, limited area.
— **be big of (someone)** to be generous of (someone).
— **the Big Apple** New York.
— **big guns** the most important people in an organization.
— **bit the big time** to be become extremely successful and famous.
— **the Big Smoke** London.

BILL

— **a clean bill of health** verification that someone is well and fit.
— **fill the bill** to be exactly what is required.
— **foot the bill** to pay for something, usually something expensive.
— **top the bill** to be the most important performer in a show.

BIND

— **bind one over** warn one that he will appear in court if he breaks the law.

BIT

— **a bit on the side** a person with whom someone is having a sexual relationship, even although he/she is already married or has a regular partner.
— **champing at the bit** very impatient.
— **take the bit between one's teeth** to act on one's own and cease to follow other people's instructions or advice.

BITE

— **bite off more than one can chew** to try to do more than one can without too much difficulty.
— **bite the bullet** to do something unpleasant but unavoidable with courage.

— **bite the dust** to die or cease to operate or function.
— **bite the hand that feeds one** to treat badly someone who has helped one.
— **have more than one bite at the cherry** to have more than one opportunity to succeed at something.
— **the biter bit** used to indicate a situation in which someone who has tried to harm or do wrong to someone has suffered in some way as a consequence of this action.

BITTER
— **a bitter pill to swallow** something unpleasant or difficult that one has to accept.
— **to the bitter end** right to the very end, however unpleasant that is.

BLACK
— **as black as one is painted** as bad as everyone says one is.
— **black sheep** a member of a family or group who is not up to the standard of the rest of the group.
— **in black and white** in writing or in print.
— **in the black** showing a profit, not in debt.

BLAME
— **to blame for** to impute fault to.

BLANK
— **blank cheque** permission to do exactly what one wants.
— **draw a blank** to fail to find out anything after much searching or research.

BLANKET
— **on the wrong side of the blanket** illegitimate.
— **wet blanket** a dull person who makes other people feel depressed.

BLAST
— **a blast from the past** someone or something that you have know in the past and is seen, heard about or suddenly brought to mind, bringing memories

of that period in the past.

BLESSING
— **a blessing in disguise** something that turns out to advantage after at first seeming unfortunate.
— **a mixed blessing** something that has disadvantages as well as advantages.

BLIND
— **fly blind** to do something without enough information and without guidance.
— **swear blind** to insist that one is telling the truth about something.
— **the blind leading the blind** referring to a situation in which the person who is in charge of others knows as little as they do.

BLINK
— **In the blink of an eye** very quickly; in a short time.
— **On the blink** not working properly; out of order.
— **Blink the fact that** ignore.
— **Blink something away/back** to try to control tears or clear the eyes by blinking.

BLOCKADE
— **break/run a blockade** get through a blockade.
— **lift a blockade** end a blockade.

BLOOD
— **bad blood** hostile feelings.
— **bay for (someone's) blood** to demand that someone is punished or held responsible for something.
— **in cold blood** deliberately and calmly.
— **like getting blood out of a stone** very difficult, almost impossible.
— **new blood** new members of an organization.
— **sweat blood** to put a very deal of effort into something.

BLOOM
— **in full bloom** (i) flowering

BLOT
— **Blot your copy book** spoil a previously good record.
— **A blot on the landscape** a thing, especially an ugly building that spoils the appearance of place.

BLOW
— **blow hot and cold** to keep changing one's mind or attitude.
— **blow over** to cease and be forgotten.
— **blow one's own trumpet** to boast about one's achievements.
— **blow the gaff** to tell something secret, often something illegal, to someone, often the police.
— **blow the whistle on (someone)** to reveal or report someone's wrongdoing so that it will be stopped.

BLOW-BY-BLOW
— **A blow-by-blow account/description** an account description in which all the details of an event are told in the order in which they happened.

BLUE
— **blue-eyed boy** a person who is someone's favourite.
— **bluestocking** an educated, intellectual woman.
— **once in a blue moon** hardly ever.
— **out of the blue** without warning.

BLUFF
— **call (someone's) bluff** to make (someone) prove that what he or she says is true is really genuine.

BLUNDER
— **to commit a blunder** to make a gross mistake.
— **blunder about/around** to move in uncertain way.
— **to blunder away** to throw away some advantage or opportunity.

BLUNT
— **to blunt the edge** to make weak or ineffectual, to weaken.

BOARD
— **go by the board** to be abandoned.
— **sweep the board** to win all the prizes.

BOAT
— **burn one's boats** to do something that makes it impossible to go back to one's previous position.
— **in the same boat** in the same situation.
— **miss the boat** to fail to take advantage of a opportunity.
— **push the boat out** to spend money in an extravagant way in order to celebrate something in a lavish way.
— **rock the boat** to do something to endanger or spoil a comfortable or happy situation.

BOB
— **Bob's your uncle** (informal)-everything is done, complete, satisfactory.
— **Bob a curtsy** curtsy quickly.

BODY
— **Body and soul** physically and mentally; completely.
— **Keep body and soul together** support life.
— **Body blow** a severe or disastrous blow.
— **Over my dead body** against my strong opposition.
— **In a body** all together.

BOGGLE
— **The mind boggles** one can hardly imagine or accept.

BONE
— **a bone of contention** a cause of dispute.
— **have a bone to pick with (someone)** to have a matter to disagree about with (someone).
— **make no bones about (something)** to have no hesitation or restraint about (saying or doing something openly).

— **near the bone** (1) referring too closely to something that should not be mentioned; tactless.
(2) slightly indecent or crude.

BOON

— **A boon companion** a cheerful friend with whom one enjoys spending time.
— **To be in someone's good/bad books** be in/out of favor with someone.
— **Throw the book at someone** reprimand.

BOOT

— **get the boot** to be dismissed or discharged from one's job.
— **give (someone) the boot** to dismiss or discharge (someone).
— **hang up one's boots** to retire from work, to cease doing an activity.
— **lick (someone's) boots** to flatter (someone) and do everything he or she wants.
— **pull oneself up by one's bootstraps** to become successful through one's own efforts.
— **put the boot in (someone)** (1) to kick (someone) when he or she is already lying on the ground injured.
(2) to treat (someone) cruelly or harshly after he or she has suffered already.
— **the boot is on the other foot** the situation has been completely turned round.
— **too big for one's boots** too conceited.

BOOTSTRAPS

— **drag/pull yourself up by your own bootstraps** improve your situation yourself, without help from other people.

BOOZE

— **Go/be on the booze** have a period of heavy drinking.

BORDER

— **border on** resemble.

— **border upon** near to.
— **border with** adjacent to.

BORN
— **a born fool** one who is a fool right from his birth.
— **not born yesterday** ignorant like a child.

BORNE
— **borne (something is), borne in upon one** one is forced to realize (something).

BORROW
— **be/live on borrowed time** live longer than the doctors expected.

BOSOM
— **bosom friend** intimate, dear friend.
— **To take to bosom** to marry, but generally make an intimate friend of.

BOTH
— **have it both ways** satisfy two demands.

BOTHER
— **bother one's head about** be anxious or concerned about.

BOTTLE
— **crack a bottle** to open a bottle.
— **hit the bottle** to drink a great deal of alcohol.
— **lose one's bottle** not to have the courage to do something or to go on with something.
— **on the bottle** drinking a great deal of alcohol regularly.

BOTTOM
— **at the bottom of (something)** the cause of (something).
— **bottom drawer** a collection of articles for the home, which a young woman gathered together before her marriage.
— **get to the bottom of (something)** to find out the exact cause of (something) or the true nature of (something).
— **hit rock bottom** to reach the lowest possible level.

— **the bottom line 1** the most important point or part of something.
2 The result or outcome.

BOUND
— **bound up in** very busy with.
— **by leaps and bound** very rapidly.
— **out of bounds** prohibited, unlawful.

BOW[1]
— **bow and scrape** to behave in a very humble and respectful way.
— **bow out** to leave or cease to take part in a project, organization, etc.
— **take a bow** to accept acknowledgment of one's achievements.

BOW[2]
— **draw the long bow** to exaggerate.
— **have another** *or* **more than one string to one's bow** to have another possibility, plan, etc, available to one.

BOX
— **to be in the box** to be in a fix.
— **box on the ears** blow on the head.

BRAIN
— **cudgel** *or* **rack one's brains** to think very hard.
— **have (something) on the** *or* **one's brain** to think or worry about (something) continuously.
— **pick (someone') brains** to find out (someone's) ideas and knowledge about a subject so that one can put them to one's own use.

BRANCH
— **to branch out or off** to spread out as a branch.
— **root and branch** thoroughly.

BRASS
— **get down to brass tacks** to consider the basic facts or issues of something.
— **the top brass** the most important people in an organization, especially originally in the army.

BRAVE

— **A brave new world** a new era from revolutionary changes.

— **put a brave face on something; put on a brave face** try to appear brave or cheerful or to be managing well in a difficult situation when in fact you are fightened or unhappy.

BRAIN

— **brain-drain** loss of educated person through emigration.

— **to blow out one's brains** to shoot to kill.

BRAND

— **brand new** completely new.

BRAZEN

— **brazen it out** show no signs of being ashamed or sorry when one is discovered doing something wrong.

BREAD

— **bread and butter** one's basic living.

— **know which side one's bread is buttered** to know the course of action that is to one's greatest advantage.

— **on the breadline** with scarcely enough money to live on.

— **the greatest thing since sliced bread** a person or thing that is greatly admired and appreciated.

BREAK

— **break even** to have one's losses balanced by one's gains, to make neither a loss nor a profit.

— **break of day** dawn.

— **make a break for it** to attempt to escape.

BREAST

— **make a clean breast of** to make a full and free confession of some secret.

— **beat one's breast** show remorse for one's mistake.

BREATH

— **catch one's breath** (1) to breathe in sharply in fear, surprise or pain.

(2) to rest for a short time.
— **hold one's breath** to wait anxiously for something.
— **save one's breath** to stop talking since one's words are having no effect.
— **take (someone's) breath away** to surprise (someone) greatly.
— **under one's breath** very quietly, in a whisper.
— **waste one's breath** to say something that is not taken heed of.

BREATHE
— **be able to breathe again** to be able to relax after a period of anxiety, etc.
— **breathe down (someone's) neck** (1) to be very close behind (someone).
(2) to be waiting impatiently for something from (someone).
— **breathe one's last** to die.

BRICK
— **drop a brick** to say something tactless or undiplomatic.
— **like a cat on hot bricks** very nervous or restless.
— **like a ton of bricks** to treat or punish (someone) severely.
— **try to make bricks without straw** to try to do something without the necessary materials or equipment.

BRIDGE
— **build bridges** to do something to help people who are in some kind of opposition to each other understand each other so that will establish a relationship or cooperate with each other.
— **cross a bridge when one comes to it** to worry about or deal with a problem only when it actually arises.

BRIEF
— **hold no brief for (someone *or* something)** not to support or defend (someone or something).

BRIGHT
— **bright-eyed and bushy-tailed** very cheerful and lively.

BRING
— **bring (someone) round** (1) to bring (someone) back from unconsciousness.
(2) to persuade (someone) to do something.

BROAD
— **have broad shoulders** to be able to accept a great deal of responsibility, criticism, etc.
— **in broad daylight** during the day.

BROTHER
— **am I my brother's keeper?** the actions or affairs of other people are not my responsibility.
— **Big Brother** a powerful person or organization thought to be constantly monitoring and controlling people's actions.

BROWN
— **in a brown study** deep in thought.

BRUSH
— **brush up on (something)** to refresh one's knowledge of (something).
— **get the brush-off** to be rejected or refused abruptly.

BUCK
— **The buck stops here** responsibility is accepted and can not be passed on somebody else.
— **Pass the buck** pass on responsibility.
— **Buck one's ideas up** become more alert.

BULK
— **bulk large** seems important; be prominent.
— **in bulk** in large amounts.

BULL
— **hit the bull's eye** to do or say something that is very appropriate or relevant.
— **like a bull at a gate** in a very unsubtle, unthinking way.
— **like a bull in a china shop** in a very clumsy way.
— **take the bull by the horns** to tackle (something) boldly.

BULLET
— **get the bullet** to be dismissed or discharged.
— **give (someone) the bullet** to dismiss or discharge (someone).

BUN
— **have a bun in the oven** be pregnant.

BUNDLE
— **a bundle of nerves** in a very nervous state.
— **go bundle on** be very fond of.

BUNK
— **do a bunk** ran away.

BUM
— **put bums on seats** to get people to go to see a play, concert, etc;

BURDEN
— **the burden of proof** the responsibility for proving something.

BURN
— **the burning question** a question of great interest to many people.

BURTON
— gone **for a Burton** dead, ruined, broken, etc.

BURY
— **burry the hatchet** stop quarrelling and become friendly.

BUS
— **busman's holiday** a holiday spent doing much the same as one does when one is at work.

BUSINESS
— **mean business** to be determined (to do something), to be serious.
— **mind one's own business** to concern oneself with one's own affairs and not interfere in those of other

people.

BUSMAN
— **a busman's holiday** holiday spent doing the some thing that one does at work.

BUST
— **go bust** to fail, to be financially ruined.

BUSY
— **busy as a bee** very busy.

BUT
— **But me no buts** don't make excuse or argue.
— **But then** on the other hand.
— **But for somebody/something** except for.

BUTCHER
— **Have/take a butcher** to have a look at something.

BUTT
— **Be the butt of something** be the person or thing that other people often joke about.

BUTTER
— **butterfingers** a person who often drops things.
— **butter (someone) up** to flatter (someone) a great deal, usually in order to get him or her to do something for one.
— **know which side of one's bread is buttered** *see* **bread.**
— **look as though butter would not melt in one's mouth** to appear very innocent, respectable, etc.

BUTTERFLY
— **have butterflies in one's stomach** to have a fluttering sensation in one's stomach as a sign of nervousness.

BUTTON
— **buttonhole (someone)** to catch (someone's) attention and engage him or her in conversation.

BUY

— **buy a pig in a poke** buy something without seeing it or knowing if it is satisfactory.
— **buy time** delay something that is about to happen.

BUZZ

— **give a buzz** make a telephone call to somebody.

BY

— **by all appearance, by all means** certainly.
— **by choice** if one could choose.
— **by dint of** because of; owing to.
— **by far** by a great amount easily.
— **By and by** before long; soon.
— **By yourself/himself** without anyone's help.
— **By the sweat of one's brow** by working very hard.
— **By the way** expression used to show that an idea or thought has just occurred to one and is not closely or logically connected to what has been talked of before.
— **By turns** first one and then the other.
— **By/in virtue of** because of (usually some good or positive thing); owing to.
— **By way of** as a means of; signifying.
— **By word of mouth** spoken, not written.

BYGONES

— **Let bygones by bygone** let s forgive and forget.

# C

CABBAGE

— **not as green as one is cabbage** looking not as foolish or inexperienced as one appears to be.

CACKLE

— **cut the cackle** stop talking trivial, unimportant matters.

CAGE

— **rattle (someone's) cage** to annoy or agitate (someone).

CAHOOTS

— **in cahoots with (someone)** forming a secret partnership with (someone), especially to do something dishonest or illegal.

CAIN

— **raise Cain** to make a great deal of noise or fuss.

CAKE

— **a piece of cake** something easy to do.

— **a slice** *or* **share of the cake** a share of something desirable or valuable.

— **cakes and ale** pleasant or enjoyable activity.

— **have one's cake and eat it** *or* **eat one's cake and have it** to have the advantages of two things or situations when doing, possessing, etc, one of them would normally make the other one impossible.

— **icing on the cake** *see* **ice.**

— **sell** *or* **go like hot** cakes to sell very quickly.

— **take the cake** *same as* **take the biscuit**-*see* **biscuit.**

CALCULATE

— **to make a calculation** to prepare an estimate.

CALL

— **call off the** dogs *see* **dog**

CALF

— **calf love** love felt by a very young, inexperienced person.
— **kill the fatted calf** to provide a lavish meal, especially to mark a celebration of someone's arrival or return.

CALL

— **answer** *or* **obey the call of nature** to go to the toilet.
— **pay a call** to go to the toilet.

CALM

— **The calm before the storm** a period of quiet before a crisis.
— **swallow a camel** to regard something as being acceptable, true, fair, etc, when it is quite clearly not so.

CAMP

— **have a foot in both camps** to have associations with two groups who have opposing and conflicting views and attitudes.

CAN

— **carry the can** to accept blame or responsibility, usually for something that someone else has done.
— **in the can** certain, agreed or decided upon.

CANDLE

— **burn the candle at both ends** to work and/or to play during too many hours of the day.
— **cannot hold a candle to (someone)** to be not nearly as good or as talented as (someone).
— **the game is not worth the candle** something that is not worth the effort that has to be spent on it.

CANOE

— **paddle one's own canoe** to control one's own affairs without help from anyone else.

CAP
— **cap in hand** humbly.
— **if the cap fits, wear it** if what has been said applies to you, then you should lake note of it.
— **put one's thinking cap on** to think very carefully about a problem.
— **set one's cap at (someone)** to try to attract (someone of the opposite sex).
— **to cap it all** on top of everything else, finally.

CAPABLE
— **capable of** being able to do.

CAPITAL
— **make capital out of (something)** to make use of (something) for one's own advantage.
— **with a capital A, B, C, etc** used to emphasize that the person or thing described is an extreme example of his, her or its kind.

CARD
— **get one's cards** to be dismissed or discharged.
— **have a card up one's sleeve** to have an idea, plan of action, etc, in reserve to be used if necessary.
— **on the cards** likely.
— **play one's cards close to one's chest** to be secretive or non-communicative about one's plans or intentions.
— **play one's cards right** to act in such a way as to take advantage of a situation.
— **put one's cards on the table** to make known one's plans or intentions.
— **stack the cards against (someone)** to make it very difficult for (someone) to succeed.

CARE
— **care of somebody** at the address of somebody.
— **have a care** be more careful.
— **take care of oneself** make sure one is safe.
— **put one in care** put in a home owned by a local authority.

CARPET

— **on the carpet** about to be rebuked or punished by someone in authority.

— **sweep (something) under the carpet** to try to hide or forget about (something unpleasant).

— **the red carpet** special, respectful treatment.

CARROT

— **carrot and stick** reward and punishment as a method of persuasion.

— **hold out a carrot to (someone)** to promise (someone) a reward in order to get him or her to do something.

CARRY

— **carry a torch for (someone)** to be in love with someone, especially with someone who does not return it.

CART

— **put the cart before the horse** to do or say things in the wrong order.

CARTE

— **be given carte blanche** to be given complete freedom to act as one wishes.

CASANOVA

— **Casanova** a man who has relationships with many women.

CASE

— **be on (someone's) case** to keep on criticizing someone or complaining about them.

CASSANDRA

— Cassandra a person who makes predictions about unpleasant future events but who is never believed.

CASH

— **out of cash** without money.

— **cash down** immediately payment of cash.

— **cash on delivery** system of paying for goods when they are delivered.

CAST

— **cast pearls before swine** to offer something valuable or desirable to someone who does not appreciate it.

— **cast the first stone** to be the first person to blame or criticize someone.

CASTLE

— **castles in the air** *or* **castles in Spain** dreams or hopes that are unlikely ever to be realized.

CATCH

— **catch (someone) in the act** to catch (someone) actually doing something wrong or bad.

— **catch it** to be scolded or punished.

— **catch (someone) napping** to surprise (someone) when he or she is unprepared or inattentive.

— **catch the sun** to become **sun**burnt or suntanned.

— **Catch 22** a situation in which one can never win or from which one can never escape, being constantly hindered by a rule or restriction that itself changes to block any change in one's plans; a difficulty that prevents one from escaping from an unpleasant or dangerous situation.

— **catch (someone) with his** or **her pants** *or* **trousers down** to surprise (someone) when he or she is unprepared or doing something wrong, especially when this causes embarrassment.

CEILING

— **go through the ceiling** to rise very high, to soar.

— **hit the ceiling** *or* **roof** to lose one's temper completely.

CEMENT

— **To cement relations** to make relations very firm.

CEREMONY

— **stand on ceremony** to behave in a formal manner.

CERTAIN

— **in a certain condition** pregnant.

CHALICE

— **hand/give (someone) a poisoned chalice** to be given something to do which seems an attractive proposition but which may well lead to failure or extreme difficulties.

CHAIN

— **the weak link in the chain** a person who does not perform as well as the others in a team.

CHALK

— **as different as chalk and cheese** completely different.

— **chalk it up to experience** accept the inevitability of something.

— **not by a long chalk** not by a long way, by no means.

CHALLENGE

— **to throw a challenge** to call on one to settle a matter by fighting or by any kind of contest.

CHANCE

— **chance it** to take a risk.

— **fancy one's chances** to think that one is highly likely to succeed.

— **have a fighting chance** to have a possibility of success if a great effort is made.

— **have an eye to the main chance** to watch carefully for what will be advantageous or profitable to oneself.

— **have a sporting chance** to have a reasonable chance of success.

— **not to have the ghost of a** chance not to have the slightest possibility of success.

— **on the off-chance (of *or* that)** in the hope (of or that), assuming there is the possibility (of or that).

— **take one's chance *or* chances** to take a risk or take advantage of an opportunity on the understanding that one accepts whatever happens.

CHANGE

— **change hands** to pass into different ownership.

— **change horses in mid-stream** to change one's opinions, plans, sides, etc, in the middle of something.

— **change one's mind** to alter one's decision or intention.

— **change one's tune** to change one's attitude or opinion.

— **chop and change** *see* **chop.**

— **have a change of heart** to alter one's opinion or decision, usually to a better or kinder one.

— **ring the changes** to add variety by doing or arranging things in different ways.

CHARACTER

— **Out of character** not in accordance with a person's usual behavior.

CHARGE

— Trump up a charge-make up a charge against someone by producing false evidence.

— Bring a charge against-formally accuse one.

— **Give one in charge** hand one over to the police.

— **Have charge of something** have responsibility for something

— **In charge of** in a position of control or command.

— **In/under one's charge** in care of somebody.

— **Lay something to somebody's charge** accuse somebody of something.

— **Take charge** take control.

CHEAP

— **To feel cheap** to be ashamed.

— **Cheap at the price** so well worth having that the price does not seem too much.

— **Hold something cheap** consider something to be of little value.

— **On the cheap** without paying the usual, or a fair price.

— **Go cheap** be offered at a low price.

CHEAT

— **Put a cheat upon** deceive.

CHECK

— **Hold/keep in check** prevent from advancing or increasing.

CHEEK
— **cheek by jowl** side by side, very close together.
— **turn the other cheek** to take no action against someone who has harmed one, thereby giving him or her the opportunity to harm one again.

CHEESE
— **cheesed off** bored, weary or dissatisfied.
— **hard cheese** bad luck, a sentiment usually expressed by someone who does not care about the misfortune.
— **say "cheese"** to smile when one has one's photograph taken.

CHESHIRE
— **grin like a Cheshire cat** to smile broadly so as to show one's teeth.

CHEST
— **get (something) off one's chest** to tell (someone) about something that is upsetting, worrying or annoying one.

CHESTNUT
— **old chestnut** an old joke, usually one no longer funny.
— **pull (someone's) chestnuts out of the fire** to rescue (someone) from a difficult or dangerous situation, often by putting oneself in difficulty or danger.

CHICKEN
— **chicken-feed** something of very little value or importance; an insignificant amount of money.
— **chickens come home to roost** misdeeds, mistakes, etc, that come back with an unpleasant effect on the person who performed the misdeed, especially after a considerable time.
— **count one's chickens before they are hatched** to make plans which depend on some thing that is still uncertain.

CHILD
— **child's play** something that is very easy to do.
— **second childhood** a time when an adult person,

often an old person, behaves like a child.
— **the child is father of the** man the character of an adult is formed from childhood influences.

CHILL
— **chill one to the bone/marrow** make one very cold.

CHIMNEY
— **smoke like a chimney** smoke cigarettes incessantly.

CHIN
— **keep one's chin up** not to show feelings of depression, worry or fear.
— **stick one's chin out** to show determination in opposing someone or something.
— **take it on the chin** to accept or to suffer (something) with courage.

CHIP
— **a chip off the old block** a person who is very like one of his or her parents.
— **cash in one's chips** to die.
— **have a chip on one's shoulder** to have an aggressive attitude and act as if everyone is going to insult or ill-treat one, often because one feels inferior.
— **have had one's chips** to have had, and failed at, all the chances of success one is likely to get.
— **when the chips are down** when a situation has reached a critical stage.

CHOICE
— **Hobson's choice** no choice at all; a choice between accepting what is offered or having nothing at all.

CHOOSE
— **Not much to choose between** each about equally bad.
— **To pick and choose** to select with care.

CHORD
— **strike a chord** to be familiar in some way.

— **touch a chord** to arouse emotion or sympathy.

CLAIM

— **Claim to fame** one thing that makes a person or place, important or interesting.

CLAMOR

— **To clamor for** to make a loud continuous demand.

CLEAN

— **a clean slate** a record free of any discredit; an opportunity to make a fresh start.

— **cleanliness is next to godliness** it is almost as important to be clean as it is to be religious and virtuous.

— **come clean** to tell the truth about something, especially after lying about it.

— **(my *or* his *or* her) hands are clean** I am or he or she is, etc, not guilty or responsible.

— **keep one's nose clean** to keep out of trouble, to behave well or legally.

— **make a clean breast of (something)** to admit to (something), especially after having denied it.

— **make a clean sweep** to get rid of everything which is unnecessary or unwanted.

CLEAR

— **clear as a bell** very easy to hear.

— **clear as crystal** very easy to understand or grasp.

— **clear as mud** not at all easy to understand or grasp.

— **clear the decks** to tidy up, especially as a preparation for some activity or project.

— **in the clear** free from suspicion.

— **steer clear of (someone *or* something)** to keep away from or avoid (someone or something).

— **the coast is clear** the danger or difficulty is now past.

CLEFT

— **in a cleft stick** unable to decide between two equally important or difficult courses of action.

CLING
— **To cling to** to hold past, to be absolutely with.

CLINCH
— **To clinch the issue** to decide the matter finally.

CLIP
— **clip (someone's) wings** to limit the freedom, power or influence of (someone).

CLOAK
— **cloak-and-dagger** involving or relating to a great deal of plotting and scheming.

CLOCK
— **against the clock** *see* **against.**
— **like clockwork** very smoothly, without problems.
— **put back the clock** *or* **turn the clock back** to return to the conditions or situation of a former time.
— **regular as clockwork** perfectly regularly.
— **round the clock** all the time; for twenty-four hours a day.

CLOSE[1]
— **behind closed doors** in secret.

CLOSE[2]
— **a close shave** something that was only just avoided, especially an escape from danger, failure, etc.
— **at close quarters** very close, from a position nearby.
— **close to home** referring to something about which someone is very sensitive or which relates very closely to someone.
— **too close for comfort** so near that one feels uncomfortable, worried, etc.

CLOUD
— **cast a cloud over (something)** to spoil (something), to introduce something unpleasant or sad into a pleasant or happy situation.
— **cloud cuckoo land** an imaginary place, where everything is perfect; an unreal world.

— **every cloud has a silver lining** something good happens for every bad or unpleasant thing.
— **have one's head in the clouds** to be day-dreaming and not paying attention to what is going on around one.
— **on cloud nine** extremely happy.
— **under a cloud** under suspicion, in trouble.

CLOVER
— **in clover** in great comfort.

CLUB
— **in the club** pregnant.
— **join the club** you are in the same unfortunate situation that I am or we are.

CLUE
— **be clued up on (something)** to be very well-informed about (something).
— **not to have a clue about (something)** to have no knowledge of (something), to be badly-informed about (something).

COACH
— **drive** a **coach and horses through (something)** to destroy (an argument etc) completely by detecting and making use of the weak points in it.

COAL
— **carry** *or* **take coals to Newcastle** to do something that is completely unnecessary, especially to take something to a place where there is already a great deal of it.
— **haul (someone) over the coals** to scold (someone) very severely.
— **heap coals of fire on** *or* **upon (someone's) head** to do good or be kind to (someone) who has done one harm so that he or she feels sorry or ashamed.
— **rake over the coals** *same as* **rake over the ashes**- *see* **ashes.**

COAT
— **cut one's coat according to one's cloth** to organize

one's ideas and aims, particularly one's financial aims, so that they are within the limits of what one has or possesses.
— **turn one's coat** to change sides.

COLD
— **cold comfort** no consolation at all.
— **come in from the cold** to be allowed to take part in some activity that one was excluded from before.
— **get cold feet** to become nervous and change one's mind about being involved in (something).
— **give (someone) the cold shoulder** to act in an unfriendly way to (someone) by ignoring him or her.
— **in a cold sweat** in a state of great fear or anxiety.
— **leave (someone) cold** to fail to impress or excite (someone).
— **make (someone's) blood run cold** to cause terror or great distress in (someone).
— **out in the cold** not taking part, not included.
— **pour** *or* **throw cold water on (something)** to discourage enthusiasm for (something).
— **stone cold** extremely cold.

COLLAR
— **A white collar job** a job in some decent office.
— **Hot under the collar** angry excited.

COLLECT
— **To collect one self** to regain, self-control.

COLOUR[1]
— **a horse of a different colour** someone or something that is completely different from someone or something else.

COLOUR[2]
— **change colour** to become either very pale or else very red in the face through fear, distress, embarrassment, anger, guilt, etc.
— **nail one's colours to the mast** to commit oneself to a point of view or course of action in a very obvious and final way.

— **off-colour** unwell.
— **show oneself in one's true colours** to reveal what one is really like after pretending to be otherwise.
— **with flying colours** with great success.

COME
— **come a cropper** to suffer misfortune, to fail.
— **come in for (something)** to be the receiver or target of (something).
— **come off it** don't be ridiculous, don't try to deceive me.
— **come to that** taking into consideration other facts.
— **come unstuck** to fail, to suffer a major setback.
— **have it coming to one** to deserve the punishment, misfortune, etc, that one is going to get.

COMMIT
— **to commit oneself to** to pledge oneself to.
— **to commit to memory** to learn by heart.

CONCERN
— Be concern in-have some connection with or responsibility for.

CONCLUSION
— **In conclusion** lastly.
— **Jump to conclusions** draw an inference from insufficient evidence.

CONDITION
— **In mint condition**-as good as new.
— **On condition that** only if.
— **On no condition** not at all.

CONFIDENCE
— **confidence trick** the act of a swindler who gains the trust of someone and then persuades him or her to hand over money.

CONFORM
— **In conformity with** in accordance with.

CONJURE
— **a name to conjure with** the name of someone very important, influential or well-known.

CONSCIENCE
— **in all conscience** being completely fair and honest.

CONTRIBUTION
— **To make a contribution** to give for a common cause.

CONTROL
— **Be in control of** be able to organize your life well and keep calm.
— **Be/get out of control** be/become no longer manageable.
— **Be under control** be being dealt with successfully.
— **Bring something under control** succeed in dealing with something so that it does not cause any harm

CONTROVERT
— **To enter into controversy** to try to refute, to try to contest.

COOL
— **cool as a cucumber** very calm and unexcited.
— **cool, calm and collected** completely calm, in full control of one's emotions.
— **cool** *or* **kick one's heels** to be kept waiting.
— **keep one's cool** to remain calm.
— **lose one's cool** to become angry, excited etc.

COOT
— **bald as a coot** *see* **bald.**

COP
— **cop it** (1) to be scolded or punished.
(2) to die.
— **not much cop** not very good, desirable, useful, etc.

COPY
— **blot one's copybook** to spoil a previously good record of behaviour, achievement, etc, by doing

something wrong.

— **carbon copy** a person or thing that is very like someone or something else.

CORD

— **cut the cord** to become independent and stop relying on someone else, such as your mother or father.

CORN

— **earn one's corn** to justify the amount of money which you earn or which has been spent on you.

— **tread on (someone's) corns** to offend (someone).

CORNER

— **cut corners** to use less money, materials, effort, time, etc, than is usually required or than is required to give a good result.

— **drive (someone) into a corner** to force (someone) into a difficult or dangerous situation.

— **from all (four) corners of the earth** from every part of the world, from everywhere.

— **in a tight corner** in an awkward, difficult or dangerous situation.

— **paint oneself into a corner** to get oneself into a difficult situation from which there is only one method of escape or action.

— **turn the corner** to begin to get better or improve.

COTTON

— **wrap (someone) in cotton wool** to be overprotective of (someone).

COUNT

— **out for the count** unconscious or deeply asleep.

COUNTER

— **under the counter** secretly or illegally.

COUNTRY

— **country cousin** a person from the country, considered unsophisticated by a town or city dweller.

— **go to the country** to hold a general election.

COURAGE

— **have the courage of one's convictions** to be brave enough to do what one thinks one should.

— **pluck up** *or* **screw up courage** to force oneself to be brave.

COURT

— **laugh (someone** *or* **something) out of court** not to give serious consideration to (someone or something).

— **pay court to (someone)** to try to gain the love of (someone).

— **the ball is in (someone's) court** it is (someone's) turn to take action.

— **rule (something) cut of court** to prevent (something) from being considered for (something).

COVENTRY

— **send (someone) to Coventry** collectively to refuse to associate with (someone).

COW

— **a sacred cow** something that is regarded with too much respect for people to be allowed to criticize it freely.

— **till** *or* **until the cows come home** for an extremely long time.

CRACK

— **a fair crack of the whip** a fair share, a fair chance of doing (something).

— **at (the) crack of dawn** very early in the morning.

— **crack the whip** to treat sternly or severely those under one's control or charge.

— **get cracking** to start moving, working, etc, quickly.

— **have a crack at (something)** to have a try at (something).

— **not all it's cracked up to be** not to be as good as it is said to be.

— **take a sledgehammer to crack a nut** to spend a great deal of effort on a small task or problem.

CRADLE

— **From the cradle** from birth, from the first.

— **From the cradle to grave**-from birth to death; from first to last; throughout.

CRAMP

— **Cramp one's style** prevent one from acting the way one would like to, or the way one normally does.

— **Be cramped for room/space** be without enough space

CRASH

— **To crash to the ground** to fall down and break into pieces; complete destruction.

— **A crashing bore** a very boring person.

CRAVE

— **To crave for** to beg for; to long for.

CREATE

— **Create a scene** cause a commotion, uproar, etc.

— **Create a sensation** make a great impression.

CREATURE

-- **creature comforts** things that contribute to one's physical well-being.

CREEK

— **up the creek** in trouble, in serious difficulties.

CREEP

— **give (someone) the creeps** to arouse dislike, disgust or fear in (someone).

— **make (someone's) flesh creep** to arouse fear or horror in (someone).

CREST

— **be (riding) on the crest of a wave** to be going through a very successful period.

CRICKET
— **lively as a cricket** very lively.
— **not cricket** not fair or honourable, unsportsmanlike.

CROCODILE
— **crocodile tears** a pretended show of grief or sorrow.

CROSS
— **cross a bridge when one comes to it** see **bridge.**
— **cross the Rubicon** to do something that commits one completely to a course of action that cannot be undone.
— **have a cross to bear** to have to suffer or tolerate a responsibility, inconvenience or source of distress.
— **talk at cross purposes** to be involved in a misunderstanding because of talking or thinking about different things without realizing it.

CROW
— **as the crow flies** measured in a straight line.
— **eat crow** to have to admit or accept that one was wrong.

CRUNCH
— **when it conies to the crunch** when a time of testing comes, when a decision has to be made.

CRY
— **a crying shame** a great shame, a disgrace.
— **a far cry from (something)** a long way from (something), very different from (something).
— **crying out for (something)** to be badly in need of something or something to be done.
— **cry over spilt milk** to waste time regretting a misfortune or accident that cannot be undone.
— **for crying out loud** a phrase used to express annoyance, impatience, etc.
— **in full cry** enthusiastically and excitedly pursuing something.

CUCKOO
— **a cuckoo in the nest** a person who gains some

kind of advantage from a situation without contributing anything useful.

CUDGEL

— **take up the cudgels on behalf of (someone** *or* **something)** to fight strongly on behalf of (someone or something), to support (someone or something) vigorously.

CUE

— **take one's cue from (someone)** to use the actions or reactions of (someone) as a guide to one's own, to copy (someone's) actions.

CUFF

— **off the cuff** without preparation.

CUP

— **not be one's cup of tea** not to be something which one likes or appreciates.
— **in one's cups** under the influence of alcohol.

CUPBOARD

— **cupboard love** pretended affection shown for a person because of the things he or she gives one.

CURATE

— **A curate's egg** thing with both good and bad aspect.

CURRY

— **curry favour with (someone)** to try to gain the approval or favour of (someone) by insincere flattery or by being extremely nice to him or her all the time.

CURTAIN

— **be curtains for (someone** *or* **something)** to be the end of (someone or something).
— **curtain lecture** a private scolding, especially one given by a wife to a husband.
— **curtain raiser** something that begins or acts as an introduction to something.

— **ring down the curtain on (something)** to cause (something) to come to an end.

CURVE

— **throw (someone) a curve** to surprise and confuse someone by doing something unexpected.

CUT

— **a cut above (someone *or* something)** rather better than (someone or something).

— **cut a long story short** to give a brief account of something quite complicated or lengthy.

— **cut and dried** settled and definite.

— **cut and thrust** methods and techniques of rivalry, argument or debate.

— **cut both** ways to have an equal or the same effect on both parts of a question or on both people involved in something.

— **cut it fine** to allow hardly enough time to do or get something.

— **cut it out** to stop doing (something).

— **cut up upset**.

— **not cut out for (something)** not naturally suited to.

# D

DAILY

— **daily bread** basic living costs.

— **daily dozen** a series of physical exercises done every day, usually every morning.

— **the daily round** the usual routine of daily life.

DAISY

— **be pushing up the daisies to** be dead.

— **fresh as a daisy** not at all tired, lively.

DAMAGE

— **what's the damage?** what does it cost? What's the total cost?.

DAMN

— **Damn with faint praise** praise someone or something, but in a way which shows that one does not like him/her it much.

— **Damn all** nothing at all.

DAMP

— **a damp squib** something which is expected to be exciting, effective, etc, but which fails to live up to its expectations.

— **put a damper on (something)** to reduce the enjoyment, optimism, happiness of (something).

DANCE

— **dance to a different tune** to act or think in a completely different way, especially when forced to do so.

— **lead (someone) a (merry) dance** to cause (someone) a series of great, usually unnecessary, problems or irritations.

DANDER

— **get one's dander up** to become very angry.

DARK

— **a leap in the dark** an action or decision, the result of which is unknown or unpredictable.

— **a shot in the dark** an attempt or guess based on very little information.

— **be whistling in the dark** to try to give the impression that you are more confident of, or less worried about, a situation than one actually is.

— **dark horse** a person or thing whose abilities, worth, etc, is unknown.

— **in the dark** lacking knowledge or awareness.

— **keep it *or* something dark** to keep it or something secret.

— **not darken (someone's) door** not to dare to visit (someone).

DAY

— **all in a day's work** all part of one's normal routine, not requiring extra or unusual effort.

— **any day of the week** whatever the circumstances.

— **at the end of the day** when everything has been taken into consideration.

— **call it a day** to put an end to (something); to stop doing (something), especially to stop working.

— **carry** *or* **win the day** to be successful, to gain a victory.

— **day in, day out** every day without exception.

— **daylight robbery** the charging of prices that are far too high.

— **(your, etc) days are numbered** you are about to be dismissed, be killed, etc.

— **don't give up the day job!** a humorous piece of advice given to someone not to stop doing his/her usual job in order to try to make a living at something which is less secure and requires a great deal of talent which the person does not have.

— **save the day** to prevent something from going wrong or from being a failure.

— **see daylight** to be coming to the end of a long task.
— **seize the day** to take advantage of any opportunities which occur now, rather than worry about the future.
— **that will be the day** that is extremely unlikely to happen.
— **the order of the day** *see* **order.**
— **the other day** one day recently.
— **those were the days** the times in the past about which we are talking were good times.

DEAD
— **a dead duck** a person or thing that is very unlikely to survive or continue.
— **a dead end** a situation from which it is impossible to progress.
— **a dead loss** a person or thing that is completely useless or unprofitable.
— **at dead of night** in the middle of the night when people are usually asleep.
— **cut (someone) dead** to ignore (someone) completely.
— **dead and buried** completely dead or extinct with no chance of being revived.
— **dead as a dodo** completely dead or out of fashion.

DEAL
— **a done deal** a project, arrangement, etc, which has been agreed to and completed and cannot be changed.
— **a raw deal** unfair treatment.
— **a square deal** fair or honest treatment.

DECISION
— **To take a decision (or) to take a final decision** to decide finally.

DECK
— **hit the deck** to fall to the ground.

DECLARE
— **Declare one's interest** reveal to others facts that might be thought to influence one's opinions or

actions on a particular issue.

DEEP
— **be thrown in at the deep end** to be put suddenly into a difficult situation of which one has no experience.
— **go off at the deep end** to lose one's temper.
— **in deep water** in great difficulties or trouble.

**DEFEND**
— **Defend against** to guard or protect.

DEPART
— **The departed soul** the dead person.

DEPEND
— **To depend on (or) upon** to rely on; to rest on.

DEPRIVE
— **To deprive of** to dispossess; to take away from someone.

DEPTH
— **in depth** thoroughly.
— **out of one's depth** in a situation which one cannot cope with.
— **plumb the depths of (something)** to reach the lowest level of unhappiness, misfortune, etc.

DESERTS
— **get one's just deserts** to be treated as one deserves, especially to receive deserved punishment.

DESIGN
— **have designs upon (someone** *or* **something)** to wish to possess (someone or something), usually belonging to someone else.

DEVICE
— **leave (someone) to his** *or* **her own devices** to leave (someone) to look after himself or herself, often after having tried unsuccessfully to help him or her.

DEVIL
— **be the very devil** to be very difficult or troublesome.

— **better the devil you know** it is preferable to have someone or something that one knows to be bad than take a chance with someone or something that might turn out even worse.
— **between the devil and the deep blue sea** faced with two possible courses of action each of which is as unacceptable as the other.
— **devil take the hindmost** the person who is last must accept the worst fate or the least acceptable conditions, so everyone should take care to avoid this position.
— **give the devil his due** to be fair to someone, even although one dislikes him or her.
— **needs must when the devil drives** if it is absolutely necessary that something must be done then one must do it.
— **play the devil's advocate** to put forward objections to a plan, idea, etc, simply in order to test the strength of the arguments in its favour.
— **speak of the devil** here is the very person whom we have just been referring to.
— **there will be the devil to pay** there will be serious trouble.

DIE[1]
— **be dying for (something)** to be longing for (something).
— **die hard** to take a long time to disappear or become extinct.
— **die laughing** to be extremely amused.
— **die with one's boots on** to die while still working.
— **never say die** never give up hope.

DIE[2]
— **the die is cast** a step has been taken which makes the course of future events inevitable.
— **On a diet** allowed to eat only some or a little food because of illness or to lose weight.

DIRT
— **dirty old man** an elderly man who shows a sexual interest in young girls or young boys.
— **dish the dirt on (someone)** to say unpleasant or

scandalous things about an individual's private life.

— **do (someone's) dirty work** to do something wrong or unpleasant on behalf of (someone else).

— **do the dirty on** (someone) to treat (someone) in an unfair, dishonest or disloyal way.

— **(someone's) name is dirt** *or* **mud** (someone) is in great disfavour.

— **treat (someone) like dirt** to treat (someone) with contempt.

DISPENSE

— **To dispense with** to do without somebody/ something.

DISTANCE

— **go the distance** to complete something successfully, to last until the end of something.

— **keep one's distance** not to come too close, not to be too friendly.

— **within striking distance** reasonably close.

DIVIDEND

— **pay dividends** to bring advantages at a later time.

DO

— **do (someone) in** to kill (someone).

— **done for** without any hope of rescue, help or recovery.

— **do or die** to make the greatest effort possible at the risk of killing, injuring, ruining, etc, oneself.

— **do (someone) out of (something)** to prevent (someone) from getting (something), usually by dishonest or deceitful means.

— **do the honours** to act as host, to serve food or drink to one's guests.

— **do time** to serve a prison sentence.

— **do (something) up** to renovate or redecorate (something).

DOCTOR

— **just what the doctor ordered** exactly what is

required.

DOG

— **a dog and pony show** an event which has been organized just to impress someone.
— **a dog in the manger** a person who stops someone else from doing or having something which he or she does not want.
— **a dog's life** a miserable life.
— **call off the dogs** to stop attacking or criticizing (someone).
— **dog eat dog** a ruthless struggle against one's rivals to survive or be successful.
— **dogs body** someone who is given all the odd jobs, particularly unpleasant ones, to do.
— **go to the dogs** to be no longer good, moral, successful, etc.
— **give a dog a bad name** if bad things are said about a parson's character they will stay with him or her for the rest of his or her life.
— **in the doghouse** in disfavour.
— **keep a dog and bark oneself** to employ someone to do a job and then do it oneself.
— **let sleeping dogs lie** do not look for trouble; if there is no trouble, do not cause any.
— **let the dog see the rabbit** let me, etc, come near, get a view, etc.
— **shaggy dog story** a very long joke with a pointless or a ridiculous ending.
— **throw (someone) to the dogs** deliberately to cause (someone) to suffer an unpleasant fate, especially when this is done for selfish or dishonest reasons.
— **top dog** the person who is in charge.
— **you can't teach an old dog new tricks** the older you get the more difficult it is to learn new skills or accept ideas or new fashions.

DONE

— **done for (informal)** in trouble.
— **done/burnt to a frazzle (informal)** overcooked; burnt.
— **done/cooked to a turn** done or made perfectly.

— **Done to death** used, made, etc. too many times.

DOUBLE
— **at the double** very quickly.
— **do a double take** to look at or think about (someone or something) a second time because one has not taken it in or understood it the first time.
— **double back** to turn round and go back the way one has come.
— **double Dutch** unintelligible words or language.
— **see double** to see two images of everything instead of one.

DOUBT
— **a doubting Thomas** a person who will not believe something without strong proof.

DOWN
— **down-and-out** (a person who is) without money or a means of support, homeless.
— **down-at-heel** untidy, uncared- for, poorly dressed.
— **down in the dumps** *or* **down in the mouth** depressed, in low spirits.
— **down the drain** completely wasted.
— **down-to-earth** very practical.
— **down under** Australia.
— **get down to (something)** to begin to work at (something) in earnest.
— **go down big** to be a great success.
— **go downhill** to get worse and worse, to deteriorate.
— **have a down on (someone** *or* **something)** to be very hostile or opposed to (someone or something).

DRAW
— **long, drawn-out** going on for a long time, especially unnecessarily.
— **out of the top drawer** from the upper classes or aristocracy.

DREAM
— **a dream ticket** used of two people who are expected

to work very successfully together.

— **dream on!** used to indicate to someone that his/her hopes of something are not likely to be realized.

— **in your dreams!** *same as* **dream on!**.

— **work like a dream** to work or operate very smoothly or successfully.

DRESS

— **dressed to kill** *or* **dressed to the nines** dressed in one's smartest clothes so as to attract attention.

DRESSING

— **dressing down** to show one's anger with somebody; to somebody.

DROWN

— **drown one's sorrows** to take alcoholic drink in order to forget one's unhappiness.

DRUM

— **drum** (someone) **out** to send (someone) away, to ask (someone) to leave.

DRY

— **a dry run** a practice attempt, a rehearsal.

— **dry** as **a bone** extremely dry.

— **dry as dust** extremely dull or boring.

— **dry up** to forget what one was going to say.

— **keep one's powder dry** to remain calm and prepared for immediate action.

— **leave (someone) high and** dry *see* **high.**

DUCK

— **a lame duck** a weak or inefficient person or organization.

— **a sitting duck** a person or thing that is very easy to attack.

— **be water off a duck's back** be totally ineffective.

— **break one's duck** to have one's first success.

— **take to (something) like a duck to water.** to be able to do (something) right from the beginning naturally and without difficulty.

— **ugly duckling** an unattractive or uninteresting person or thing that develops in time into someone or something very attractive, interesting or successful.

DUTY

— **duty bound** required by one's duty.

DWELL

— **to dwell on (or) upon** to speak or think at some length.

DYE

— **dyed-in-the-wool** thorough, of firmly fixed opinions.

— **dying** *see* **die.**

# E

EAGER

— **eager for** keen for.

— **eager in** keen in doing.

— **Eager beaver** someone who is very enthusiastic.

EAR

— **bead (someone's) ear** to keep talking to someone for a long time so that you annoy or bore him/ her.

— **be out on one's ear** to have to leave a job, organization, etc..

— **give one's ears for (something)** *same as* **give one's right arm for (something)** *see* **arm.**

— **go in one ear and out the other** not to make any tasting impression.

— **grin from ear to ear** to have a wide smile on your face.

— **have nothing between the ears** to be stupid.

— **have (someone's)** ear to have the sympathetic attention of (someone, usually someone influential).

— **have (something) coming out of one's ears** used to emphasize how much of something you have.

— **have** *or* **keep one's ear to the ground** to keep oneself informed about what is happening around one.

— **listen to (someone or some-thing) with only half an ear** not to pay much attention to what is being said.

— **(my, etc) ears are burning** someone somewhere is talking about (me, etc).

— **pin back one's ears** to listen attentively.

— **pin back (someone's) ears** to reprimand (someone).

— **play it by ear** to deal with matters as they arise without making plans beforehand.

— **prick up one's ears** to begin to listen attentively.
— **up to one's ears in (something)** deeply involved in (something).

EASY
— **easy as Tailing off a log** *or* **easy as pie** extremely easy.
— **easy meat** someone or something that is easily taken advantage of.
— **easy on the eye** very attractive.

EAT
— **be at the cutting edge of (something).** to be involved in the most modern, advanced development or stage of (something).
— **have (someone) eating** out **of one's hand** to have (someone) doing everything that one wishes, because he or she likes or admires one.
— **what's eating you?** what's annoying or troubling you?.

EGG
— **be left with egg on** one's face to be left looking foolish.
— **put all one's eggs in one basket** to rely entirely on the success of one project, etc.
— **teach one's grandmother to suck eggs** to try to tell someone how to do something when he or she is much more experienced than oneself at it.
— **you can't make an omelette without breaking eggs** *see* **omelette**.

ELEMENT
— **in one's element** in a situation in which one is happy or at one's best.

ELEPHANT
— **a white elephant** something which is useless and troublesome to look after.
— **have a memory like an elephant** never to forget things.
— **see pink elephants** to have hallucinations,

especially when one has drunk too much alcohol.

ELEVENTH

— **at the eleventh hour** at the last possible minute.

END

— **at a loose end** with nothing to do, with no plans.
— **at the end of one's tether** at the end of one's patience, tolerance, etc.
— **keep one's end up** to perform as well as other people involved.
— **make ends meet** to live within the limits of one's income.
— **the end justifies the means** if the result is good it does not matter how one achieved it.
— **the end of the line** *or* **road** the point beyond which survival is impossible.

ENOUGH

— **enough is as good as a feast** if you have enough of something you should be satisfied with that; you do not need any more.

ENTER

— **to enter into** to become a party to.
— **enter on** to be in.
— **enter upon** to engage in.
— **to enter the field** to come forward, to complete.
— **enter somebody's head** be thought of by somebody; occur to somebody.
— **enter sb's/your name for something** apply for a place at a school, in a competition etc for somebody or yourself.
— **enter the lists against one**-challenge one or accept a challenge.

ERROR

— **see the error of your ways** to realize or admit that one has done something wrong or behaved badly.

ESCAPE

— **Escape literature** light reading.

— **Escape one' notice** be missed or not noticed.
— **Make good one's escape** manage to escape completely and satisfactorily.

ESSENCE

— **of the essence** of the greatest importance.

ETERNAL

— **eternal rest** death.
— **eternal triangle** a sexual relationship between two men and one woman or between two women and one man.
— **the Eternal City** Rome.

EVEN

— **get even with (someone)** to be revenged on (someone).
— **get** *or* **keep on an even keel** to be or keep steady or calm with no sudden changes.

EVENT

— **be wise after the event** to realize how a situation should have been dealt with after it is over.
— **in the event** as it happened.
— **in the event of (something)** if (something) happens.

EXPENSE

— **at the expense of (someone** *or* **something)** causing loss, harm, embarrassment, etc.

EXPERT

— **To be expert in**-skilled in any art.

EXPOSE

— **To be exposed to** to lay forth; to view; to lay bare.

EXTREME

— **to go extremes**-to go too far; to use extreme measures.
— **in the extreme** in the last; highest degree.

EYE

— **all my eye (and Betty Martin)** completely untrue.

— **an eye for an eye (and a tooth for a tooth)** a punishment to match the offence committed.
— **a sight for sore eyes** a pleasant or welcome sight.
— **a smack in the eye for (someone)** an insult or rebuff for (someone).
— **be one in the eye for (someone)** to be something unpleasant that happens to someone who deserves it.
— **can** see **with half an eye** to see or understand without difficulty.
— **close one's eyes to (something)** deliberately to ignore (something blameworthy).
— **cry one's eyes out** to weep bitterly.
— **eye-opener** something which reveals an unexpected fact.
— **eyesore** something extremely ugly.
— **feast your eyes on (something)** to look at (something) with a great deal of pleasure.
— **get your eye in** to get some practise or experience at doing something so that you become more skilful.
— **have an eye for (someone *or* something)** to be a good judge of (someone or something), to be able to spot (someone or something) as a good example.
— **in the twinkling of an eye** very rapidly, immediately.
— **keep an eagle eye on (someone or something)** to watch (someone or something) extremely closely.
— **keep a weather eye open *or* keep one's eyes peeled *or* skinned** to keep a close watch, to be alert.
— **make eyes at (someone)** to look at (someone) with sexual interest.
— **not to bat an eyelid** not to show any surprise, distress, etc.
— **open (someone's) eyes to (something)** to make (someone) aware of (something, usually unpleasant) previously unknown.
— **raise some/a few eyebrows** to surprise or shock some people.
— **see eye to eye with (someone)** to be in agreement with (someone).
— **the evil eye the** supposed power of causing harm

by a look.

— **there's more to (someone** *or* **something) than meets the eye** the true worth or state of (someone or something) is not immediately obvious.

— **turn a blind eye to (something)** *same as* **close one's** eyes **to (something)** *see* ***above.***

— **with one's eyes open** fully aware of one's actions.

EYEBALL

— **eyeball to eyeball**-to face to face.

EYE-TOOTH

— **cut one's eye-teeth**-acquire experience in the ways of the world.

— **give one's eye-tooth for**-wish to possess or obtain something very much.

# F

FABIAN
— **a fabian policy** a dilatory policy, delaying tactics.

FACE
— **face the music** to face and deal with a situation caused by one's actions.
— **fly in the face of (something)** to oppose or defy (something).
— **get out of (someone's) face** to go away and stop annoying (someone).
— **give (something) a face-lift** to make (something) look better, to renovate (something).
— **have a long face** to look unhappy.
— **have a face like thunder** to be very angry-looking.
— **in the face of (something)** while having to cope with (something unpleasant).
— **keep a straight face** to stop oneself from smiling or laughing.
— **lose face** to suffer a loss of respect or reputation.
— **make** *or* **pull a face** to twist one's face into a strange or funny expression.
— **put a brave face on it** to try to appear brave when one is feeling afraid, distressed, etc.
— **save (someone's) face** to prevent (someone) from appearing stupid or wrong.
— **set one's** face **against (someone** *or* **something)** to oppose (someone or something) with great determination.

FACTS
— **facts of life** information about facts.
— **as a matter of fact** in reality.
— **matter of fact** to the point and practical.

FADE
— **to fade away** to lose freshness or colour gradually.

FAINT
— **faint heart never won fair lady** boldness is necessary to achieve what one desires.
— **not to have the faintest** not to have the slightest idea.

FAIRY
— **be away with the fairies** to be crazy or out of one's mind so that one imagines things.
— **a fairy godmother** a person or organization that offers unexpected help with a problem or difficulty.

FAITH
— **in (all) good faith** with honest and sincere intentions.

FALL
— **fall about** to be extremely amused.
— **fall back on (someone *or* something)** to rely on (someone or something) if all else fails.
— **fall down on (something)** to do badly at (something).
— **fall flat** to fail, to have no effect.
— **fall foul of (something *or* something)** to do something that arouses someone's anger or *hostility.*
— **fall from grace** to lose (someone's) favour.

FALSE
— **under false pretences** by using deceit.

FAMILIARITY
— **familiarity breeds contempt** people cease to appreciate people or things they know well.

FAMILY
— **in the family way** pregnant.
— **run in the family** to be a characteristic found in many members of the same family.

FANCY
— **(footloose and) fancy free** not in love with anyone,

not romantically attached.
— **take** *or* **tickle one's fancy** to attract one, to arouse a liking in one.

FAR
— **far and away** by a very great amount.
— **far be it from** (someone) to (someone) has no right to do something.
— **go far** to be very successful.
— **go too far** to do or say something that is beyond the limits of what is acceptable.
— **so far, so good** up until now the project, etc, has been successful.

FATE
— **a fate worse than death** something terrible that happens to one, often rape.
— **seal (someone's) fate** to ensure that something, usually unpleasant, happens to (someone).
— **tempt fate** to act in a way that is likely to bring one ill luck or misfortune.

FATHER
— **the father and mother of (something)** an extreme example of (something, usually something bad).

FAULT
— **to a fault** to too great an extent.

FAUX
— **make/commit a faux pass** an action or a remark that causes embarrassment because it is not socially correct.

FEAR
— **put the fear of death** *or* **God into (someone)** to terrify (someone).
— **there is no fear of (something)** it is not likely that (something) will happen.
— **without fear or favour** with complete fairness.

FEEL
— **feel free** to do what you wish.

— **feel in one's bones** to know (something) by instinct.
— **feel one's feet** to be becoming used to a situation.

FEET
— **at (someone's) feet** (1) easily within (someone's) reach or power.
(2) greatly admiring of (someone).
— **drag one's feet** to take a long time to do something.
— **fall** *or* **land on one's feet** to be fortunate or successful, especially after a period of uncertainty or misfortune.
— **find one's feet** to become capable of coping with a situation.
— **have feet of clay** to have a surprising weakness, despite having been thought to be perfect.
— **have both feet on the ground** or have one's feet on the ground to be practical and sensible.
— **get under (someone's) feet** to hinder or get in (someone's) way.
— **put one's feet up** to take a rest.
— **sit at (someone's) feet** receive tuition from (someone) and be influenced by (him or her).
— **stand on one's own feet** to **be** independent.
— **sweep (someone) off his** *or* **her feet** to affect (someone) with great enthusiasm or emotion; to influence (someone) to do as one wishes.

FEMME
— **be a femme fetale** be a beautiful woman that men find sexually attractive but who brings them trouble or unhappiness.

FENCE
— **mend fences** to put things right after a quarrel, etc.
— **rush one's fences** to act too hurriedly or rashly.
— **sit on the fence** to refuse to take sides in a dispute, etc.

FETCH
— **Fetch and carry for somebody**-be always doing small jobs for sb; as if you were sb's servant.

FETTLE
— **In fine/good fettle**-healthy and cheerful.

FEVER
— **At fever pitch**-in a state of great excitement or great activity.

FEW
— **A good few**-a considerable number.
— **Have had a few**-have drunk a lot of alcohol.
— **A man/woman of few words**-a person who does not talk much.
— **Few and far between**-very rare, unusual.

FIDDLE
— **fit as a fiddle** extremely fit.
— **play second fiddle to (someone)** to be in a subordinate or inferior position to (someone).

FIELD
— **have a field day** to have a very busy, successful or enjoyable day.
— **play the field** to take advantage of many chances offered to one, especially to go out with several members of the opposite sex.

FIGURE
— **figure head** a head (of state) without powers of administration.

FILE
— **in single/Indian file** in a line, one person after another.

FILL
— **fill a dead man's shoes** *same as* **step into a dead man's shoes**
— **fill out** to get plumper.
— **have had one's fill** to have had enough, to be unable to tolerate any more.

## FIND

— **find out the hard way** to find out (something) by one's own experience rather than from others.

## FINDERS

— **finders keepers (losers weepers)** (expression often used by children when they find something) the person who finds something is entitled to keep it.

## FINE

— **get (something) down to a fine art** to have learned to do (something) extremely well.
— **go through (something) with a fine-tooth comb.** to search (something) very carefully.

## FINGER

— **be all fingers and thumbs** to be clumsy or awkward when using one's hands.
— **burn one's fingers** *or* **get one's fingers burnt** to suffer because of something that one has been involved in.
— **cross one's fingers** to hope for good fortune.
— **get** *or* **pull one's finger out** to stop wasting time and get on with something.
— **have a finger in every pie** to be involved in a large number of projects, organizations, etc.
— **have a finger in the pie** to be involved in something.
— **have (something) at one's fingertips** to know all the information about (something).
— **let (something) slip through one's fingers** to lose (an advantage, opportunity, etc), often by one's inaction.
— **not to lift a finger** not to do anything at all.
— **point the finger at (someone)** to indicate who is to blame.
— **put one's finger on (something)** to identify (something) exactly.
— **twist** *or* **wrap (someone) round one's little finger** to be able to get (someone) to do exactly as one wishes.
— **work your fingers to the bone** to work extremely

hard.

FINISH

— **To give the finishing touch**-to complete.

FIRE

— **be breathing fire** to be extremely angry.
— **fight fire with fire** to use the same kind of methods as one's opponent.
— **get on like a house on fire** to get on very well.
— **hang fire** to wait or be delayed.
— **have many** *or* **several irons in the fire** see **iron.**
— **hold one's fire** to delay doing something.
— **in the firing line** in a situation in which you are likely to be blamed or criticized.
— **light a fire under** (someone) to make (someone) start working harder or more energetically.
— **play with fire** to take tasks, to do something dangerous.
— **set the Thames** *or* **world on fire** to do something remarkable.
— **under fire** being attacked.
— **would** go **through fire for (someone)** used to emphasize what lengths someone would go to for a loved one.

FIRST

— **at first hand** directly.
— **first thing** early in the morning or in the working day.
— **get to** *or* **make** *or* **reach first base** *see* **base.**
— **in the first flush of (something)** in the early and vigorous stages of (something).
— **not to know the first thing about (something)** to know nothing about (something).
— **of the first water** of the highest quality, of the most extreme type.

FISH

— **a fishing expedition** an attempt to get information or find out the truth about something, often in a secretive way.

— **a queer fish** a person who is considered strange or eccentric.
— **fish in muddy** *or* **troubled waters** to concern oneself with matters that are unpleasant or confused.
— **have other fish to fry** to have something else to do, especially something that is more important or more profitable.
— **like a fish needs a bicycle** used to emphasize how unnecessary someone or something is.
— **like a fish out of water** ill at ease and unaccustomed to a situation.
— **like shooting fish in a barrel** used with reference to some kind of contest or competition in which one side is so much stronger than the other that the weaker side has no chance of winning.
— **there's plenty more fish in the sea** many more opportunities will arise; many more members of the opposite sex are around.

FLAME
— **an old flame** a former boyfriend or girlfriend.
— **fan the flames** to make a difficult situation worse.

FLASH
— **a flash in the pan** a sudden, brief success.

FLAT
— **in a flat spin** in a state of confused excitement.

FLAVOUR
— **flavour of the month** a person or thing that is particularly popular at a particular time, although this is likely to be temporary.

FLEA
— **a flea in one's ear** a sharp scolding.
— **flea-market** a market where second-hand or cheap clothes and goods are sold.

FLESH
— **a thorn in (someone's) flesh** a permanent source of annoyance or irritation.

— **flesh and blood** (1) family, relations.
(2) human beings in general.
— **get** *or* **have one's pound of flesh** to obtain everything that one is entitled to, especially if this causes difficulties or suffering to those who have to give it.
— **in the flesh** in real life, not in a photograph.
— **the flesh-pots** luxurious living.

FLIES
— **Die/drop/fall like flies**-die, become ill, etc. in large numbers.
— **There are no flies on sb**-sb is skilful or clever at doing something.

FLIGHT
— **A flight of fancy**-an idea or a statement that is very imaginative but not practical or sensible.
— **In the first/top flight** among the best of a particular group.
— **Take flight**-run away.

FLING
— **Fling out**-to act or speak recklessly.
— **Full fling**-at the utmost speed, recklessly.
— **Have a fling**-have a short sexual relationship with somebody.

FLOOD
— **before the flood** a very long time ago.

FLY[1]
— **a fly in the ointment** something that spoils something.
— **there are no flies on (someone)** there is no possibility of deceiving or cheating (someone), there is no lack of sense in (someone).
— **would like to be a fly on the wall** would like to be present and able to hear what is going on without being seen.

FLY[2]
— **be dropping like flies** used to emphasize that a

great number of people are becoming ill or dying from the same cause.
— **be flying high** to be very successful, to be in a position of power.
— **get off to a flying start** to have a very successful beginning.

FOOT
— **follow in (someone's) footsteps** to do the same as someone else, particularly a relative, has done before.
— **get off on the wrong foot** to get off to a bad or unfortunate start.
— **have one foot in the grave** to be very old.
— **put one's foot down** to be firm about something, to forbid someone to do something.
— **put one's foot in it** to do or say something tactless.
— **shoot oneself in the foot** to make a make a mistake or do something stupid which causes problems for oneself or harms one's chances of success.

FOR
— **a for B**-comparing A with B.
— **for all**-in spite of.
— **for a song**-very cheaply.
— **for good (and all)**—for ever.
— **for good measure**-in addition.
— **for sure**-without any doubt; with certainty.
— **for that matter**-in connection with that.
— **for the asking/taking**-if you want to ask for (take) it.
— **(strictly) for the birds** (informal)-not true (at all); believed only by foolish people.
— **for the high jump** (informal)-going to be punished in some way.
— **for the life of one** (used for emphasis)-really.
— **for want of**-owing to the lack of.
— **for goodness'/heaven's/sake** exclamation to show surprise or annoyance.
— **(not) For love or money**-(not) for any reason.
— **for one thing**-to give one reason.

— **for one's part**-in one's opinion, speaking for oneself.
— **for short**-a shorter, quicker way of naming someone or something.

FORCE
— **force someone's hand**-make someone do something he/she doesn't want to do.
— **bring sth/come into force**-(cause a law, rule, etc. to) start being used.
— **force the issue**-do something to make people take action quickly.
— **force of circumstances**-a situation in which you are forced to do sth by factors beyond your control.
— **force of habit**-a tendency always to do things in a certain way because you have always done them in that way.
— **force the pace**-make somebody do sth more quickly or make sth happen more quickly.
— **a force to be reckoned with**-a person or thing that has a lot of power and influence and should therefore be treated seriously.

FORE
— **be/come to the fore**-be or become important and noticed by people; play an important part.
— **bring sth to the fore**-make sth become important and noticed by people.

FOREGONE
— **foregone conclusion**-opinion formed before arguments or investigation.

FORK
— **speak with a forked tongue** to tell lies.

FORM
— **be good *or* bad form** be in or not in accordance with social conventions or customs.
— **on form** in good condition, fit and in a good humour.
— **true to form** in accordance with someone's usual pattern of behaviour.

FORT

— **hold the fort** to take temporary charge of something.

FROG

— **have a frog in one's throat** to be hoarse.

FRUIT

— **forbidden fruit** something desirable that is made even more so because one is forbidden for some reason to obtain it.

FRY

— **out of the frying pan into the fire** free of a difficult or dangerous situation only to get into a worse one.

FULL

— **be full of oneself** to be very conceited.
— **full of beans** active; lively, in good spirits.
— **in full** completely, with nothing left out.
— **in the fullness of time** when the proper time has arrived, eventually.

FUN

— **fun and games** a lively time, an amusing time.
— **make fun of (someone)** *or* **poke fun at (someone)** to laugh at (someone), to make mocking remarks about (someone).

FUSS

— **make a fuss** to complain vigorously.
— **make a fuss of (someone)** to pay a lot of attention to (someone), to show (someone) a lot of affection.
— **the gift** of **the gab** the ability to talk readily and easily. *He loves public speaking. He has the gift of the gab.*

# G

GAIN

— **gain ground** to make progress, to become more generally acceptable or popular.

— **gain time** to arrange things so that one has more time to do something.

GALLERY

— **play to the gallery** to act in an amusing or showy way to the ordinary people in an organization, etc, in order to gain popularity or their support.

GALLOP

— **gallop through**-to make rapid progress.

GAMBLE

— **take a gamble on**-gamble.

— **gamble on sth/ doing sth**-to act in the hope of sth by gambling.

GAME

— **beat (someone) at his *or* her own game** to do better than (someone) at his or her activity, especially a cunning or dishonest one.

— **be on the game** to be a prostitute.

— **give the game away** to reveal a secret plan, trick, etc, usually accidentally.

— **play games** not to treat something seriously enough.

— **play the game** to behave fairly and honourably.

— **stay ahead of the game** to be able to deal successfully with any changes that may occur in an activity in which one is involved.

— **the game is up** the plan, trick, crime, etc, has been discovered and so has failed.

GAMUT
— **Run the gamut of**-experience or perform the complete range of.

GARDEN
— **everything in the garden is lovely** everything is fine.
— **lead (someone) up the garden path** to mislead or deceive (someone).

GASP
— **at one's last gasp** just about to collapse, be ruined, die, etc.

GET
— **be getting on for (something)** to be close to (a particular age, time, etc).
— **get nowhere** to make no progress.
— **tell (someone) where to get off** to tell (someone) that one will not tolerate him or her or his or her behaviour anymore.

GHOST
— **give up the ghost** to die, stop working, etc.
— **lay a ghost/lay the ghost of (something)** to do something which stops you any longer from being affected by or upset by something which happened in the past.

GIFT
— **be in one's gift** if something is in (someone's) gift then that person has the right or power to give it to anyone.
— **look a gift horse in the mouth** to criticize something that has been given to one.

GLANCE
— **glance one's eyes down/over/through something**-take a very quick, superficial look at something.
— **at first glance/sight**-when seen or examined for the first time.
— **give sb away**-to lead bride to the bridegroom and hand her to him.

GLARE

— **the glare of publicity**-constant attention from newspapers, television, etc..

GLASS

— **glass ceiling** an invisible barrier, established by tradition, personal discrimination, etc. which prevents women from achieving the top jobs in their companies, professions, etc.

— **people who live in glass houses should not throw stones** people with faults themselves should not criticize faults in others.

GLEAM

— **a gleam of somebody's eye**-person or thing that is expected at sometime in future but is thought about with pleasure or desire.

GLOSS

— **gloss over** to avoid facing unpleasant facts by giving them only a cursory description or omit them altogether.

— **put a gloss on (something)** to elaborate on a subject in a falsely flattering way.

GLOVE

— **fit like a glove** to fit perfectly.

— **handle (someone** *or* **something) with kid gloves** *see* **kid.**

— **take the gloves off** to begin to fight, argue, etc, in earnest.

GO[1]

— **from the word go** right from the very start.

— **give (someone** *or* **something) the go-by** to ignore or disregard (someone or something).

— **have a go** (1) to make an attempt.

(2) to try to stop a criminal escaping from the scene of a crime.

— **make a go of it** *or* **something** to make a success of something.

— **no go** impossible, not given approval.

— **on the go** continually active, busy.

GOAL

— **score an own goal** to do something which fails to achieve what you set out to do and, instead, harms your own interests.

GOALPOST

— **move the goalposts** to change the conditions, rules or aims applying to a project, etc after it is under way so that it disadvantageous to others but advantageous to oneself.

GOAT

— **act the goat** to behave in an intentionally silly way.

— **get (someone's) goat** to irritate (someone).

GOD

— **a little tin god** a person who thinks that he or she is more important than he or she is and tries to order others around.

— **in the lap of the gods** uncertain, left to chance or fate.

— **there but for the grace of God go I** if I had not been fortunate that could easily have happened to me.

— **think one is God's gift to (someone)** to have a very conceited opinion of oneself.

GOLD[1]

— **be sitting on a goldmine** to posses something very valuable or potentially profitable, often without realizing this.

— **like living in a goldfish bowl** in a situation where one has very little privacy.

— **strike gold** to do or find something that makes one very rich or very successful.

GOLD[2]

— **a gold mine** a source of wealth or profit.

— **be like gold dust** be very scarce.

— **golden boy** a young man who is popular or successful.

— **golden handshake** a large amount of money given to someone who is leaving a job, usually because he or she has been declared redundant.
— **good as gold** very well-behaved.
— **the crock** *or* **pot of gold at the end of the rainbow** wealth or good fortune that one will never achieve.
— **the golden rule** a principle or practice that it is vital to remember.
— **worth its** *or* **one's weight in gold** extremely valuable or useful.

GONE
— **gone on (someone)** very much attracted to (someone).

GOOD
— **a good job** a satisfactory or fortunate state of affairs.
— **all to the good** to one's benefit or advantage.
— **be as good as one's word** to do what one has promised do.
— **be on to a good thing** *or* **have a good thing going** to be in a desirable or profitable situation.
— **be up to no good** to be planning something wrong or illegal.
— **for good (and all)** for ever, permanently.
— **give as good as one gets** to be as successful as one's opponent in an argument, contest, fight, etc.
— **take (something) in good part** to accept (something) without being offended or angry.

GOODS
— **deliver the goods** to do what one is required or expected to do.
— **goods and chattels** movable property.

GOOSE
— **cook (someone's) goose** to ruin (someone's) chances of success.
— **kill the goose that lays the golden egg** to destroy something that is a source of profit or advantage to oneself.
— **what's sauce for the goose is sauce for the gander**

what applies to one person should apply to another, usually to a member of the opposite sex.

GOOSEBERRY
— **play gooseberry** to be the third person present with a couple who wish to be alone.

GRACE
— **in (someone's) good graces** to be liked by or be popular with (someone), often because one has done him/her a favour of some kind.
— **saving grace** a good quality which prevents someone or something from being completely bad or worthless.
— **with a bad** *or* **good grace** in an unpleasant or pleasant and unwilling or willing way.

GRADE
— **make the grade** to succeed in what you are trying to achieve, often by reaching a required standard.

GRAIN
— **go against the grain** to be against someone's inclinations, feelings or wishes.

GRAPE
— **sour grapes** saying that something that one cannot have is not worth having.
— **the grapevine** an informal and unofficial way of passing news and information from person to person, gossip.

GRAVE
— **(someone) would turn in his** *or* **her grave** (someone) would be very annoyed or upset.

GRAVY
— **the gravy train** an easy method of getting a great deal of money or other advantages.

GREEK
— **be all Greek to me, etc, I,** etc, don't understand any of it.
— **Greek gift** a gift that is dangerous or

disadvantageous to the person given it.
— **the Greek calends** never.

GREEN
— **give the green light to (something)** give one's permission for (something).
— **green about the gills** looking as though one were going to be sick.
— **have green fingers** to be good at growing plants.

GREY
— **a grey area** a part of a subject, etc, where it is difficult to distinguish between one category and another, an area of confusion.
— **grey matter** brain, powers of reasoning.

GRIEF
— **come to grief** to suffer misfortune or failure.
— **give (someone) grief** to criticize or nag *(someone).*

GRIST
— **it's all grist to the** *or* **someone's mill** all this experience, information will prove useful in some way.

GROUND
— **fall on stony ground** to have no attention paid to it.
— **get in on the ground floor** to be in at the very start of a project, business, etc.
— **get (something) off the ground** to get (a project) started.
— **hit the ground running** to start a new activity immediately with a great deal of energy and enthusiasm.
— **ground rules** basic rules which must be obeyed or applied.
— **run oneself into the ground** to become exhausted from working too hard or trying to do too many things.
— **run (someone** *or* **something) to ground** *same as* **run (someone** *or* **something) to earth** *see* **earth.**
— **shift one's ground** to change one's opinions, attitude, etc.

— **stand one's ground** to remain firm, not to yield.

— **suit (someone) down to the ground** to suit someone perfectly.

— **take /occupy the moral high ground** to adopt a position based on the fact that you feel your opinions, policies or actions are morally superior to those of others.

GUARD

— **let your guard down/lower your guard/drop your guard** to stop being careful or alert.

— **on** *or* **off one's guard** prepared or unprepared for any situation, especially a dangerous or difficult one.

GUESS

— **your guess is as good as mine** I have no idea.

GUINEA

— **guinea pig** a person who is the subject of an experiment.

GULLET

— **stick in one's gullet** *same as* **stick in one's throat** (*see* **throat**).

GUM

— **gum up the works** to cause a machine, system, etc, to break down.

— **up a gum tree** in a very difficult or hopeless situation.

GUN

— **be gunning for (someone)** to plan to harm (someone).

— **big guns** *see* **big.**

— **go great guns** to be going or performing very well.

— **hold a gun to (someone's) head** *same as* **hold a pistol to (someone's) head** (*see* **pistol**).

— **jump the gun** to start before the proper time.

— **spike (someone's) guns** to cause (someone's) plans or actions to be ineffective.

— **stick to one's guns** to remain firm in one's opinions, etc.

— **with all/both guns** blazing fiercely and aggressively.

# H

HABIT

— **make a habit/practice of sth**-do sth regularly.
— **fall/get into bad habits**-acquire bad habits.
— **habit of mind**-mental constitution.

HAIR

— **get in (someone's) hair** to irritate (someone).
— **keep one's hair on** to remain calm and not get angry.
— **let one's hair down** to behave in an informal, relaxed manner.
— **make (someone's) hair stand on end** to terrify or horrify (someone).
— **not to turn a hair** not to show any sign of fear, distress, etc.

HALE

— **Hale and hearty**-(especially of old people) strong and healthy.

HALF

— **(someone's) better half** (someone's) wife or husband.
— **do things by half** to do things in an incomplete, careless way.
— **go halves with (someone)** to share costs with (someone).
— **half a loaf is better than no bread** a little of something desirable is better than nothing.
— **meet (someone) halfway** to reach a compromise agreement with (someone).

HALVES

— **Do nothing/not do anything by halves**-do whatever you do completely and thoroughly.

— **Go halves with somebody**-share the total cost of sth equally with somebody else.

HAND

— **at** *or* **on hand** available, ready for use, ready to help.
— **close at hand** very near.
— **force (someone's) hand** to force (someone) to do something that he or she may not want to do or be ready to do.
— **give** *or* **lend (someone) a (helping) hand** to help (someone).
— **go hand in hand** to be closely connected.
— **hand (something) down** to pass (something) from one generation to another.
— **hand over fist** in large amounts, very rapidly.
— **have a hand in (something)** to be involved in (something), to have contributed to the cause of (something).
— **have one's hands full** to be very busy.
— **keep one's hand in** to retain one's skill at something by doing it occasionally.
— **know (someone** *or* **something) backwards** *or* **like the back of one's hand** *see* **back.**
— **lend (someone) a hand** to help (someone).
— **live from hand to mouth** to have enough money only to pay for one's present needs without having any to save.
— **many hands make light work** a job is easier to do if there are several people doing it.
— **play into (someone's) hands** to do exactly what someone wants one to do because it is to his or her advantage.
— **put one's hand in one's pocket** to spend or give money.
— **show one's hand** to reveal to others one's plans or intentions, previously kept secret.
— **take (someone) in hand** to train or discipline (someone).
— **throw in one's hand** to give up, to abandon a course of action, etc.
— **turn one's hand to (something)** to do, to be able to do.

— **with one hand tied behind one's back** very easily.

HANDLE
— **fly off the handle** to lose one's temper.

HANG
— **a hanging matter** a very serious subject or deed.
— **get the hang of (something)** to learn how to do (something) or begin to understand (something).
— **hang one's head** to look ashamed or embarrassed.

HAPPY
— **go to the happy** hunting **ground** to die.
— **happy as a lark** *or* **sand-boy** extremely happy.
— **happy event** the birth of a baby. *When is the happy event?*
— **happy hunting ground** a place where someone finds what he or she desires or where he or she is successful.
— **the** *or* **a happy medium** a sensible middle course between two extremes;

HARD
— **be hard put to it (to do something)** to have great difficulty (in doing something).
— **give (someone) a bard time** to act in an unpleasant, unsympathetic or tough way towards (someone).
— **hard-and-fast** not to be changed or ignored.
— **hard as nails** lacking in pity, sympathy, softer feelings, etc.
— **hard-bitten** tough, toughened by experience of life.
— **hard-boiled** not influenced by emotion.
— **hard cash** coins and banknotes as opposed to cheques, etc.
— **hard done by** unfairly treated.
— **hard facts** facts that cannot be disputed.
— **hard-headed** practical and not influenced by emotion.
— **hard lines** bad luck.

HARE
— **run with the hare and hunt with the hounds** to try to give one's support to two opposing sides at once.

— **start a hare** to raise a subject in the course of a discussion, often to divert attention from what was the main subject of it.

HARM

— **come to harm**-be injured physically, mentally or morally.
— **do more harm than good**-have an effect which is more damaging than helpful.
— **out of harm's way**-in a safe place.
— **there is no harm in (somebody) doing something**-used to say sb that something is a good idea and will not cause any problems.
— **no harm done**-used to tell somebody not to worry because they have caused no serious damage or injury.

HAT

— **hang up one's hat** to move into a house, job, etc, with the intention of staying a long time.
— **hats off to (someone)** (someone) should be praised and congratulated.
— **hat trick** any action done three times in a row.
— **I'll eat my hat** an expression used to express total disbelief in a fact, statement, etc.
— **keep (something) under one's hat** to keep (something) secret.
— **knock (someone *or* something) into a cocked hat** to defeat or surpass (someone or something) completely.
— **pass the hat round** to ask for contributions of money.
— **take one's hat off to (someone)** to express or show one's admiration for someone).
— **talk through one's hat** to talk about something without any knowledge about it, to talk nonsense.
— **throw one's hat in the ring** to declare oneself a contender or candidate for something.
— **wear a different *or* another hat** to speak as the holder of a different position.

HATCH

— **batten down the hatches** to prepare for trouble.
— **hatches, matches and despatches** the

announcement of births, marriages and deaths in a newspaper.

HAVE

— **have had it** to have no hope of survival, success, etc.

— **have it in for (someone)** to try to cause trouble for (someone).

— **have it in one** to have the ability, courage, etc, to do something.

— **have it out with (someone)** to discuss areas of disagreement or discontent with someone in order to settle it.

— **have (someone) on** to try to deceive (someone), often for a joke.

— **let (someone) have it** suddenly to attack (someone) either physically or verbally.

HEAD

— **bite** *or* **eat** *or* **snap (someone's) head off** to speak very sharply and angrily to (someone).

— **bring (something) to a head** to bring something to a state where something must be done about it.

— **bury one's head in the sand** to deliberately ignore a situation so that one does not have to deal with it.

— **have a head for (something)** to have an ability or aptitude for (something).

— **have a (good) head on one's shoulders** to be clever or sensible.

— **have one's head screwed on the right way** to be sensible.

— **head over heels** completely.

— **heads will roll** someone is going to get into serious trouble.

— **hit the headlines** to attract a great deal of media attention.

— **hold one's head up (high)** not to feel ashamed or guilty, to remain dignified.

— **keep a level head** *or* **keep** ones **head** to remain calm and sensible, especially in a difficult situation.

— **lose one's head** to cease to remain calm, to act foolishly.

— **make headway** to make progress.
— **need one's head examined** to be foolish or insane.
— **not to know whether one is** on **one's head** *or* **one's feet** *or* **heels** to be totally confused.
— **off one's head** insane, not rational.
— **off** the **top of one's head** *see* **top.**
— **on (someone's) (own) head be it** (someone) must take responsibility or blame.
— **rear its ugly head** to appear or happen.
— **scratch one's head** to be puzzled.
— **soft** *or* **weak in the head** not very intelligent, mentally retarded.
— **talk one's head off** to talk a great deal.
— **turn (someone's) head** to make (someone) conceited.

HEART
— **a heart-to-heart** a private talk where one tells one's thoughts, troubles, etc, openly.
— **at heart** basically, really.
— **break (someone's) heart** to make (someone) very sad.
— **cross one's heart** said to emphasize the truth of what one is saying.
— **do (someone's) heart good** to give (someone) pleasure.
— **eat one's heart out** to be distressed because one cannot have someone or something which one is longing for.
— **learn something by heart** to memorize (something) thoroughly.
— **lose heart** to grow discouraged.
— **not to have the heart (to do something)** not to be unkind, unsympathetic, etc, enough (to do something).
— **put new heart into (someone)** to make (someone) feel encouraged and more hopeful.
— **set one's heart on** *or* **have one's heart set on (something)** to desire (something) very much.
— **take heart** to become encouraged.
— **take (something) to heart**
— **warm the cockles of the heart** to make one feel happy and contented.
— **wear one's heart on one's sleeve** to let one's

feelings be obvious.
— **with all one's heart** most sincerely.

HEAT
— **in the heat of the moment** while influenced by the excitement or emotion of the occasion.
— **take the heat out of (something)** to make (a situation) less emotional, tense, etc.

HEAVE
— **give (someone) the (old) heave-ho** to get rid of (someone), to dismiss (someone).

HEN
— **like a hen on a hot girdle** very nervous and restless.

HERE
— **neither here nor there** of no importance.
— **the hereafter** life after death.

HIDE
— **neither hide nor hair of (someone *or* something)** no trace at all of (someone or something).
— **on a hiding to nothing** in a situation where one cannot possibly win.
— **tan (someone's) hide** to beat or thrash (someone).

HIGH
— **a high flier** a person who is bound to be very successful or who has achieved great success.
— **be for the high jump** to be about to be punished or scolded.
— **be high time** be time something was done without delay.
— **be *or* get on one's high horse** to be or become offended in a haughty manner.
— **high and mighty** arrogant.
— **high spot** an exceptionally good part of something.
— **hunt *or* search high and low for (someone *or* something)** to search absolutely everywhere for (someone or something).

HIKE
— **take a hike**-a rude way of telling sb to go away.
— **hike something up**-to pull or lift something up,

especially one's clothing.

HILL

— **over the hill** past one's youth or one's best.

HINT

— **Take a/the hint**-understand what somebody wants you to do, even though they tell you in an indirect way.

HISTORY

— **be history** to be past, to be no longer relevant or important.
— **make history** to do something remarkable that will be remembered in the future.
— **the rest is history** used to indicate that no more need be said about something because the details of it are well known.

HITCH

— **hitch your wagon to a star**-try to succeed by forming a relationship with sb/sth that is already successful.

HITCHED

— **get hitched**-get married.

HITHER

— **hither and thither**-in many different directions.

HOLD

— **have a hold over (someone)** to have power or influence over (someone).
— **hold (something) against (someone)** to dislike (someone) because of (something) he or she has done.
— **hold forth** to talk for a long time forcefully or pompously.
— **hold good** to be valid or applicable.

HOLY

— **holier-than-thou** acting as though one is more moral, more pious, etc, than other people.
— **the holy of holies** a private or special place inside a building.

## HOME

— **a home from home** a place where one feels comfortable and relaxed.
— **bring** *or* **drive (something) home to (someone)** to cause someone fully to understand or believe (something).
— **do one's homework** to prepare thoroughly for a meeting, etc, by getting all the necessary information.
— **feel at home** to feel comfortable and relaxed.
— **home and dry** having successfully completed an objective.
— **home truth** a plain, direct statement of something that is true but unpleasant or difficult for someone to accept.
— **make oneself at home** to make oneself comfortable and relaxed.
— **nothing to write home about** not very special, not remarkable.
— **romp home** to win easily.

## HONEST

— **Earn/turn an honest penny**-earn by fair means.
— **Honest** to **God/ goodness**-truthfully.
— **Make an honest woman of sb**-marry a woman who you have been having a sexual relationship with;

## HOPE

— **great white hope** someone or something that is expected to bring victory, fame, glory, etc, to a group.
— **have high hopes of (something)** to be extremely hopeful of success in (something).
— **hope against hope** to continue to hope although there is little reason to be hopeful.
— **hope springs eternal (in the human breast)** it is of the nature of human beings to hope.
— **pin one's hopes on (someone** *or* **something)** to rely on (someone or something) helping one in some way.

## HORN

— **draw in one's horns** to restrain one's actions, particularly the spending of money.
— **horn in on (something)** to join in on (something)

uninvited and unwanted.
— **lock horns** to argue or fight.

HORROR
— **horror of horrors**-used to emphasize how bad a situation is.

HORSE
— **back the wrong horse** to show support for the person, side, plan, etc, that turns out to be the loser in some way.
— **eat like a horse** to eat a great deal.
— **flog a dead horse** to continue to try to arouse interest, enthusiasm, etc, in something which is obviously not, or no longer, of interest.
— **hold one's horses** not to move so fast.
— **horse sense** common sense, practicability.
— **horses for courses** certain people are better suited to certain tasks or situations.
— **willing horse** someone who is keen to work or help.

HOT
— **have the hots for (someone)** an informal way of saying that someone is sexually attracted to someone.
— **hotline** a direct telephone line for use in emergencies.
— **hot on (someone's) heels** close behind (someone).
— **hot potato** something which it is difficult or dangerous to deal with.
— **hot under the collar** angry or agitated.
— **in hot water** in trouble.
— **in the hot seat** in a position where one has responsibility for important and difficult issues.
— **make it** *or* **things hot for (someone)** to make a situation unpleasant or impossible for (someone).
— **piping hot** very hot.

HUDDLE
— **get/go into a huddle (with sb)** move close to somebody so that you can talk about something without other people hearing.

— **huddle up (against/ to sb/sth)** to curl one's body up into a small space

HUMBLE

— **eat humble pie** to have to admit that one has been wrong.

HUMP

— **be over the hump** to have got past the worst part of a difficult situation.

— **get the hump** to become annoyed, offended or upset.

HUNDRED

— **a hundred/ thousand/ million and one (things, etc. to do)**-very many or too many things to do

HUNKERS

— **on your hunkers**-sitting on your heels with your knees beat up in front of you.

HUNGRY

— **go hungry**-remain unfed.

# I

IDEA

— **get the idea** understand.

— **have (got) not idea** not have the first, slightest idea, not know sth at all; not know how to do sth at all.

— **the (very) idea** used to express surprise of disapproval at the way somebody behaves.

— **that's an ideal** used to reply in a positive way to a suggestion that somebody has made.

— **run away with the idea that** be misled by or accept a false idea.

IF

— **if and when** used to say sth about an event that may or may not happen.

— **if I were you; if I was/were in your shoes/place** used to introduce a suggestion or piece of advice.

— **if only** used to express to wish that something had happened or would happen.

— **ifs and/or buts**-used to stop somebody arguing, protesting or making excuses when you tell them to do something.

ILLUSION

— **be under an/the illusion**-believe wrongly.

IMAGE

— **be the spitting image of** *or* **the spit and image of (someone** *or* **something)** *see* **spit.**

IMPRESSION

— **be under the impression that**-have the (usually mistaken) idea that.

IMPULSE

— **on impulse suddenly and without**-previous

thinking or planning.

IN
— **be in for (something)** to be likely to experience (something, often something unpleasant).
— **be in on (something)** to be involved in (something), to know about (something).
— **be in with (someone)** to be friendly with or in favour with (someone).
— **the ins and outs of (something)** the details of (something).

INFORMATION
— **for your information**-used to tell sb that they are wrong about sth.

INITIATIVE
— **on one's own initiative**-without anyone else ordering one to do something, or suggesting that one should do it.
— **take the initiative**-take the first step in an undertaking, especially one that encourages other to act.

INNINGS
— **have a good innings** to enjoy a considerable period of life, success etc.

INS
— **the ins and outs (of something)** all the details of sth, which are often difficult to understand.

INSIDE
— **inside out**-with the part that is usually inside facing out
— **on the inside**-within a group or an organization so that one has direct access to information, etc.

IRON
— **have many** *or* **several irons in the fire** to be involved in several projects, etc, at the same time.
— **rule (someone** *or* **something) with a rod of iron** to rule with the sternness or ruthlessness.

— **strike while the iron is hot** to act at a point at which things are favourable to one.
— **the iron hand in the velvet glove** sternness or ruthlessness hidden under an appearance of gentleness.
— **the iron horse** railway engines or trains'.

ISSUE
— **(The point, etc.) At issue** the most important of the subject that is being discussed.
— **Make an issue (out) of the something** behave as if something is more serious or important than it really is
— **Take issue with somebody (about/on/over something)** disagree and argue with sb about sth.

ITEM
— **be an item** to be regarded as having a romantic relationship.

# J

JACK

— **a jack of all trades (and master of none)** someone who can do several different kinds of job (but does not do any of them very well).

— **a jack in office** a pompous, dictatorial official.

— **all work and no play makes Jack a dull boy** *see* **work.**

— **before you can say Jack Robinson** extremely rapidly.

— **every man jack** absolutely everyone.

— **I'm all right, Jack** my situation is satisfactory, the implication being that it does not matter about anyone else.

JEKYLL

— **a Jekyll and Hyde** someone with two completely different sides to his or her personality.

JEST

— **In jest**-as a joke, not seriously

JET

— **the jet set** wealthy people who can afford to travel a great deal.

JEWEL

— **the jewel in the crown** the must valuable or successful thing associated with someone or something.

JOB

— **a job lot** a mixed collection.

— **give (something) up as a bad job** to stop doing (something) because one has little hope of success.

— **have a job** to have difficulty.

— **just the job** exactly what is required.

JOE

— **Joe Bloggs** *or* **Public** *or* **Soap** the ordinary, average person.

JOG

— **Jog somebody's memory** help somebody to remember sth.

— **Jog along/on** to continue in a steady manner.

JOKE

— **be no joke** to be a serious matter.

— **beyond a joke** no longer amusing, rather serious or annoying.

— **crack a joke** to make a funny remark, to tell a funny story.

JOY

— **full of the joys of spring** very happy and cheerful.

— **no joy** no success, no luck.

JUMP

— **a jumping-off point** a place from which to begin.

— **be** *or* **stay one jump ahead** to be or keep slightly ahead of someone or something in some way.

— **get/have the jump on (someone)** to start something before someone else does and so have an advantage.

JURY

— **the jury is still out** people have not yet reached a conclusion or made a decision about something.

JUST

— **just so** very neatly arranged.

# K

KEEP

— **keep in with (someone)** to remain friendly with (someone) or in (someone's) favour.

— **keep it up** to carry on doing something as well as one is doing it.

— **keep on at (someone)** to urge (someone) constantly to do something, to nag (someone).

KICK

— **for kicks** for thrills or fun.

— **get a kick out of** to get fun or a thrill out of something.

— **kick oneself** to be annoyed with oneself.

— **kick over the traces** to defy rules that control one's behaviour.

— **kick the bucket** *see* **bucket.**

— **kick (someone) upstairs** to appoint (someone) to a job which is more senior than the present one but which has less power.

KID

— **handle (someone** *or* **something) with kid gloves** to deal with (someone or something) very tactfully or delicately.

— **the new kid on the block** the newest person in a place, activity, etc..

KILL

— **be in at the kill** to be present when something important or decisive happens, often something that is unpleasant for someone.

— **move in for the kill** to act decisively with a view to defeating one's opponent.

KIND
— **of a kind** of poor quality.

KINDLY
— **Not take kindly to somebody/something** find it difficult to accept sb/sth.

KITE
— **fly a kite** to start a rumour about a new project to see how people would react if the project were put into operation.
— **high as a kite** very excited.

KNIFE
— **have one's knife in (someone)** to wish to harm (someone).
— **like a (hot) knife through butter** used to emphasize how easily someone has dealt with a difficult situation.
— **on a knife edge** in a very uncertain or risky state.
— **stick the knife in (someone)** to do something that will harm, upset or cause problems for (someone).
— **the knives are out for (someone)** used to describe a situation in which several people are planning to harm or cause problems for (someone).
— **the night of the long knives** a time when an act of great disloyalty is carried out, usually by the sudden removal of several people from power or employment.

KNOB
— **with knobs on** used to indicate that something or someone is an extreme example of something.

KNOT
— **at a rate of knots** extremely rapidly.
— **tie the knot** to get married.
— **tie (oneself *or* someone) in knots** to get (oneself or someone) in a confused state.

KNOW
— **in the know** knowing facts, etc, that are known

only to a small group of people.

— **know (something) backwards** *or* **like the back of one's hand** *see* **back.**

— **know (something) inside out** to know and understand (something) very well indeed.

— **not to know one is born** to lead a trouble-free, protected life.

# L

LABOUR

— **a labour of love** a long or difficult job done for one's own satisfaction or from affection for someone rather than for reward.

— **to labour with** to take pains to convince.

— **hard labour** sentence of hard work imposed on criminals during imprisonment.

— **lost labour** work without any achievement or result.

— **to labour under** to be oppressed; to be in travail.

LACK

— **lack all** one who is destitute.

— **lack luster** not conspicuous, wanting brightness.

LACONIC

— **a laconic speech** a short pithy speech.

LAID

— **To be laid up with** to be confined to bed due to sickness.

LAM

— **on the lam** escaping from somebody, especially from the police.

LAMB

— **like a lamb to the slaughter** meekly, without arguing or resisting, often because unaware of danger or difficulty.

LANGUAGE

— **speak the same language** to have similar tastes and views.

LAST[1]

— **as a** *or* **in the last resort** when all other methods have failed.

— **have the last word** to make the last or decisive statement in an argument, etc.

— **on one's** *or* **its last legs** near to collapse.

— **the last straw** *same as* **the straw that breaks the camel's back** *see* **straw.**

— **the last word** the most fashionable or up-to-date example of something.

LAST[2]

— **stick to one's last** to continue to do the job that one is experienced in.

LATITUDE

— **To give latitude** to give free hand.

LAUGH

— **have the last laugh** to be victorious or proved right in the end, especially after being scorned, criticized, etc.

— **laugh and the world laughs with you (weep and you weep alone)** when someone is cheerful or happy, other people share in his or her joy (but when he or she is sad or miserable, people tend to avoid him or her).

LAW

— **be a law unto oneself** to behave as one wishes rather than obeying the usual rules and conventions.

— **lay down the law** to state one's opinions with great force, to give orders dictatorially.

— **take the law into one's own hands** to take action against a crime or injustice without involving the police or courts.

— **the law of the jungle** the unofficial rules for survival or success in a dangerous or difficult situation where civilized laws are not effective.

LEAD[1]

— **a leading question** a question asked in such a way as to suggest the answer the questioner wants to hear.

— **to lead one by nose** to make one do what you want.

— **leading light** an important person in a certain group, field, etc.
— **lead somebody astray** encourage somebody to behave in silly or criminal way.
— **to lead away** to take away.
— **to lead aside from**-to deviate from.
— **lead (someone) a dog's life** miserable, be unhappy, cause (someone) to be unhappy, miserable.
— **lead someone a merry chase/dance** avoid being caught or found by someone (over a long distance, period of time).
— **lead from the front** take an active part in what you are telling or persuading others to do.

LEAD[2]
— **swing the lead** to avoid doing one's work usually by inventing deceitful excuses.

LEAF
— **take a leaf out of (someone's) book** to use (someone) as an example.
— **turn over a new leaf** to change one's behaviour, etc, for the better.

LEAGUE
— **be in league with (someone)** to have joined together with (someone), usually for a bad purpose.
— **not be in the same league as (someone)** not to be as able as (someone).

LEARN
— **learn your lesson**-learn what (not) to do in the future because you have had a bad experience in the past.

LEASE
— **give (someone** *or* **something) a new lease of life** to cause (someone) to have a longer period of active life or usefulness or to have a happier or more interesting life.

LEAVE
— **leave (someone) in the lurch** to leave (someone) in a difficult or dangerous situation without any help.

— **leave** *or* **let well alone** to make no change to something that is already reasonably satisfactory.

LEG

— **break a leg** used as an interjection to an actor or other stage performer as a means of wishing him/ her good luck.

— **get one's leg over** especially of a man, to have sex with someone.

— **give (someone) a leg up** to give (someone) some assistance to achieve advancement.

— **have hollow legs** to be able to drink a great deal of alcohol.

— **have legs** to be likely to be successful or to work.

— **leg it** to run or go away quickly.

— **not to have a leg to stand on** to have no defence or justification for one's actions.

— **pull (someone's) leg** to try as a joke to make (someone) believe something that is not true.

— **stretch one's legs** to go for a walk.

LEGEND

— **a legend in one's own lifetime** used to indicate that someone has become famous during his/ her lifetime.

— **a legend in one's own lunch time** used humorously to indicate that someone has been famous for a very short time.

LENGTH

— **go to great lengths** to take absolutely any action in order to achieve what one wants.

LETTER

— **the letter of the law** the exact wording of a law, rule, agreement clause.

— **to the letter** in every detail.

LEVEL

— **a level playing field** a situation which is completely fair to all involved and in which no one has any particular advantage.

— **find one's *or* its (own) level** to find out what situation, position, etc, one is naturally suited to.
— **on the level** honest, trustworthy.

LICK
— **a lick and a promise** a quick, not thorough, wash or clean.
— **lick (someone *or* something) into shape** to improve (someone or something) greatly to bring up to standard.

LID
— **blow *or* take the lid off (something)** to reveal the truth about (something).
— **keep the lid on (something)** to keep (something) secret or keep (something) under control so that it does not get any worse.
— **put the (tin) lid on (something)** to finish (something) off usually in an unpleasant way.

LIE[1]
— **give the lie to (something)** to show that (something) is untrue.
— **lie in *or* through one's teeth** to tell lies obviously and unashamedly.
— **live a lie** to live a way of life about which there is something dishonest.

LIE[2]
— **lie heavy on (someone)** to be a burden or source of anxiety to (someone).
— **take (something) lying down** to accept an unpleasant situation without protesting or taking action against it.
— **the lie of the land** the nature and details of a situation.

LIFE
— **breathe new life into (something)** to make (something) more lively, active or successful.
— **come to life** to become active or lively.
— **get a life** used to indicate to someone that you

think that he/she has a boring, uninteresting life and should do something to change this.

— **get on with your own life** used as a cliche to advise someone to forget about the past and concentrate on the future.

— **life is just a bowl of cherries** used ironically to indicate that life can be difficult and unpleasant.

— **for dear life** *or* **for dear life's sake** to a very great extent, very rapidly, hard, etc.

— **for the life of me** if my life depended on it.

LIKE

— **like a bat out of hell** (informal)-very fast; very quickly.

— **like a shot** very quickly.

— **to feel like** to be disposed to do anything.

— **(sell) Like hot cakes (be sold)** very quickly.

— **like it or lump it** (informal)-put up with, endure something, whether one lies it or not.

— **like made/like blazes/like anything very much** very quickly, very strongly, etc..

— **(spend) Like water (spend)** freely.

— **Like water off a duck's back** without any effect.

— **(spend) Like wildfire** (spead) very quickly.

— **The likes of** a person like people like (often used in a critical way).

LILY

— **be lily-livered** to be cowardly.

LIMB

— **out on a limb** in a risky and often lonely position; having ideas, opinions, etc, different from other people.

— **tear (someone) from limb to limb** to attack (someone) in a fierce and aggressive way, either in deed or speech.

LINE

— **all along the line** at every point in an action, process, etc.

— **along** *or* **on the lines of (something)** similar to

(something).

— **be in line for (something)** to be likely to get (something).

— **be/come on line** to be ready for use, to be operating.

— **be (way) out of line** to behave in a way that is not acceptable.

— **bring (something) into line with (something)** to make (something) the same as or comparable with (something else).

— **cross the line** to start behaving in a way which is unacceptable, offensive or extreme.

— **down the line** some time in the future.

— **draw a line under (something)** to regard (something unpleasant) as being over and best forgotten so that people can move on.

— **draw the line** to fix a limit.

— **drop (someone) a line** to send (someone) a short letter.

— **fall into line** to behave according to the relevant rules. Regulations or traditions.

— **lay it on the line** to make (something) absolutely clear to someone.

— **lay** *or* **put (something) on the line** to risk losing (something).

LIST

— **enter the lists** to join in a contest or argument.

LIVE[1]

— **beat** *or* **knock the living daylights out of (someone)** to give (someone) a severe beating.

— **live and let live** to get on with one's own life and let other people get on with theirs without one interfering.

— **live it up** to have an enjoyable and expensive time.

LIVE[2]

— **a live wire** an energetic, enthusiastic person.

LONE

— **a lone wolf** someone who prefers to be alone.

LONG

— **in the long run** in the end, after everything has

been considered.
— **the long and the short of it** the only thing that need be said, to sum the story up in a few words.

LOOK
— **look askance at (someone *or* something)** to regard with disapproval or distrust.
— **look before you leap** give careful consideration before you act.
— **look down on (someone)** to regard and treat (someone) as being inferior.
— **look in on (someone)** to pay (someone) a brief visit, usually without prior notice or invitation.
— **look (someone) up and down** to look at someone carefully and critically.
— **look up to (someone)** to regard (someone) with great respect or admiration.

LOOSE
— **cut loose** to free oneself from the influence of power of (someone or something).
— **hang loose** used to suggest to someone that he/she try to relax and remain calm about something.
— **on the loose** enjoying freedom and pleasure.

LORD
— **drunk as a lord** extremely drunk.
— **live like a lord** to live in rich and luxurious way.
— **lord it over (someone)** to act in a proud and commanding manner to (someone).

LOSE
— **lose ground** to Jose one's advantage or strong position.

LOSS
— **cut one's losses** not to spend any more time, money or effort on something on which one has already spent a lot to little benefit.

LOST
— **(a) Lost cause** something that must fail.

LOVE

— **not for love nor money** not in any way at all.
— **there's no love lost between them** they are hostile to each other.

LOW

— **keep a low profile** not to draw attention to oneself or one's actions or opinions.
— **lie low** to stay quiet or hidden.
— **the low-down** information, especially of a secret or damaging nature.

LUMP

— **in lump sum**-the whole amount together.
— **to have a lump in one's throat** to be ready to weep.
— **lump in one's throat**-feeling of great emotion, e.g. sadness or pride.

# M

MAD

— **mad as a hatter** utterly insane, extremely foolish or eccentric.

— **mad as a March hare** insane, silly, extremely eccentric.

MADE

— **made of money** very wealthy.

— **made-to-measure** (with reference to clothes)-cut to fit the person who is to wear it

— **made to order**-made according to what someone wishes or requires.

MAIDEN

— **maiden speech** the first speech made as a member of the British House of Commons.

— **maiden voyage** the first voyage undertaken by a ship.

MAKE

— **make as if to (do something)** to act as if one were about to (do something).

— **on the make** trying to make a profit for oneself.

MAP

— **put (somewhere) on the map** to cause (somewhere) to become well-known or important.

MARBLE

— **have marbles in one's mouth** to speak with an upper-class accent.

— **lose one's marbles** to become insane or senile.

MARCH

— **get one's marching orders** to be told to leave, to be

dismissed.

— **steal a march on (someone)** to gain an advantage over (someone) by doing something earlier than expected.

MARE

— **a mare's nest** a supposed discovery of something which turns out to be imaginary or completely different from what was expected.

MARINE

— **tell that to the marines I** do not believe you.

MARK

— **be a marked man** or **woman** to be in danger or trouble because people are trying to harm one.

— **beside** *or* **wide of the mark** off the target or subject.

— **be up to the mark** to reach the required or normal standard.

— **get off one's mark** to get started quickly on an undertaking.

— **hit the mark** to be correct or accurate.

— **leave one's mark on (someone** or **something)** to have an important and lasting effect on (someone or something).

— **make one's mark** to make oneself well-known, to make a lasting impression.

— **overstep the mark** to do or say something which is unacceptable or offensive.

— **quick off the mark** quick to act.

MARKET

— **be in the market for (something)** to be interested in buying (something).

MATTER

— **a matter of life or death** something of great urgency, something that might involve loss of life.

— **as a matter of course** as part of a routine.

— **be the matter** be the problem, be what is wrong.

MEAL
— **make a meal of (something)** to treat (something) as it is more complicated or time-consuming than it is.

MEANS
— **by all means**-certainly.
— **by any means**-in any way.
— **by no means**-certainly not.
— **by fair means or foul-by** hook or by crook, any how.

MEET
— **meet one's Waterloo** to be finally defeated.

MERIT
— **to merit**-to have the right to claim as a reward.
— **order of merit**-place in a class or list in which the best is placed first, the next, best next and so on.

MERRY
— **make merry** to have an enjoyable, entertaining time, to have a party.
— **merry-andrew**-one who makes sport for others, a clown
— **merry go round**-a revolving ring or hobby horses, etc. on which children ride round at fairs; etc.

MIGHT
— **with might and main** with maximum strength and power.

MIND
— **be** *or* **go out of one's mind** to be or become insane.
— **blow (someone's) mind** to *amaze,* (someone), to excite (someone) greatly.
— **cross one's mind** to enter one's mind briefly.
— **give (someone) a piece of one's mind** to scold or criticize (someone) angrily.
— **great minds think alike** clever people tend to have the same ideas and opinions.
— **have a good mind to (do something)** to feel inclined

to (do something).
— **have a mind of one's own** to form one's own opinions, to be independent.
— **have half a mind to (do something)** to feel slightly inclined to (do something).
— **in one's right mind** sane, rational.
— **in two minds** undecided.
— **make up one's mind** to reach a decision.
— **a mine of information** a rich or productive source of information.

MISTAKE
— **and no mistake** without any doubt.

MIX
— **to mix up**-to confuse
— **to mix up with**-to mingle with; to associate with.
— **mixed marriage**-marriage in which the contracting persons are of different religions
— **mixed blessing**-something that has bad effects as well as good.

MOMENT
— **have one's moments** to have times of success, happiness.
— **not for a moment** not at all.
— **the moment of truth** a crucial time, a time when one has to make an important decision, face a crisis, etc.

MONEY
— **be in the money** to be well off, sometimes temporarily.
— **be right on the money** to be completely right.
— **for my money** in my opinion, as my choice.
— **have money to burn** to have enough money to be able to spend it in ways considered foolish.
— **money for jam** *or* **old rope** money obtained in exchange for very little work, effort, etc.
— **money talks** rich people have influence simply because they have money.
— **put one's money where one's mouth is** to give

money for a cause or purpose which one claims to support.

— **spend money like water** to spend money very freely.

— **the smart money is on (something)** used to describe an event or situation which is very likely to take place.

— **throw good money after bad** to spend money in an unsuccessful attempt to retrieve money which one has already lost.

— **throw money at (something)** to spend a lot of money on something, when this will not necessarily help, rather than spend time and effort on solving the problem or improving the situation by more helpful means.

— **you pays your money and you takes your choice** used to indicate the difficulty or impossibility of deciding which of two choices is the right one.

MOTHER

— **a mother's** *or* **mummy's boy** a boy or man who depends too much on his mother; a weak, effeminate boy or man.

— **mother's milk** something that one needs or enjoys very much.

MOTION

— **go through the motions** to make a show of doing something, to pretend to do something.

MOULD

— **be in the same as mould as (someone)** to have the same good qualities or talents as (someone).

— **break the mould** to do something in a completely new and better way.

— **cast in the same mould (as someone)** very similar (to someone).

— **they broke the mould when they made (someone)** used to emphasize how special or exceptional someone is.

MOUNTAIN

— **have a mountain to climb** used to emphasize how difficult it is going to be for someone to do or achieve something and how much effort will be needed.

— **if the mountain will not come to Mohammed, then Mohammed must go to the mountain** a saying which indicates that, if someone whom you want to see cannot or is unwilling to come to you, then you should make the effort to go to him/ her. Often shortened to **if the mountain will not come to Mohammed,** it being assumed that the rest of the saying will be understood. It is also found in the form of **Mohammed must go to the mountain.**

— **make a mountain out of a molehill** greatly to exaggerate the extent of a problem, etc.

— **move mountains** to achieve something that seems impossible or extremely difficult.

MOUSE

— **poor as a church mouse** extremely poor.

— **quiet as a mouse** extremely quiet.

MOUTH

— **be all mouth and trousers** to talk a lot about doing something but never actually do it.

— **have a big mouth** to talk a lot, especially about things, such as secrets, that one should not.

— **out of the mouths of babes and sucklings** used when a child says something that is surprisingly adult, true, wise, etc.

— **shoot one's mouth off** to talk in a loud and often boastful or threatening manner.

— **make one's mouth water** used to emphasize how delicious something smells or looks.

MOVE

— **get a move on** to hurry.

— **make the first move** to be the person who acts first, especially in a situation where two people are romantically or sexually attracted to each other.

— **not to be able to move for (something)** used to emphasize how much of something there is or how many people there are.

MUCH

— **make much of (someone *or* something)** to pay

(someone or something) a great deal of attention.
— **make much of (something)** to treat (something) as being of great importance.
— **much ado about nothing** a great fuss about something very minor.
— **much of a muchness** very similar.
— **not much of a (something)** not a very good (something).
— **not up to much** not very good.
— **without so much as** without even.

MUCK
— **muck in** to join in a task, etc.
— **muck-raking** searching for scandalous information, usually with the intention of publishing it.
— **where there's muck there's brass** where there is dirt and ugliness in a place there is often industry and so wealth.

MUD
— **drag (someone/someone's reputation) through the mud** to damage (someone or someone's reputation) by saying bad things about him/her.
— **here's mud in your eye!** a rather old-fashioned drinking toast to wish someone well.
— **mud sticks** used to indicate that, if something bad is said about someone, some people are likely to believe this and to go on believing it, even if it is not at all true or if it has been disproved.
— **(someone's) name is mud** (someone) is in disfavour or is being criticized.
— **sling** *or* **throw mud at (someone** *or* **something)** to say bad or insulting things about (someone or something).

MUG
— **a mug's game** something that only foolish people would involve themselves in.

MUSIC
— **be music to one's ears** used to indicate that one is very pleased to hear something.

MUSTARD
— **keen as mustard** very eager and enthusiastic.
— **not cut the mustard** not to be able to do or achieve something; not be good enough.

MUSTER
— **pass muster** to be considered good enough.

MUTTON
— **mutton dressed as lamb** an older person, usually a woman, dressed in clothes suitable for young people.

# N

NAIL
— **a nail in (someone's) coffin** something which helps to bring about (someone's) downfall or destruction.
— **hit the nail on the head** to be extremely accurate in one's description, judgement, etc, of someone or something.
— **pay (something) on the nail** to pay (something) immediately.

NAME
— **be (someone's) middle name** used to emphasize how typical of someone something is.
— **call (someone) names** to apply insulting or rude names to (someone).
— **clear (someone's) name** to prove that (someone) was not involved in a crime or misdeed of which he or she was accused.
— **give (someone *or* something) a bad name** to damage the reputation of (someone or something).
— **in name only** not in practice.
— **make a name for oneself** to become famous or well-known.
— **name-dropping** the habit of mentioning the names of famous or important people as though they were friends.
— **name names** to give the names of people, especially people who are guilty or accused of wrong-doing.
— **no names, no pack-drill** no names will be mentioned and so no one will get into trouble.
— **the name of the game** the important or central thing.

NATURE
— **the nature of the beast** the basic typical feature

or quality of someone or something.

NEAR

— **a near miss** something unpleasant that very nearly happened, often the near collision of two planes in the sky.

— **a near thing** the act of just avoiding an accident, misfortune, etc.

— **one's nearest and dearest** one's close family.

NECK

— **be in (something) up to one's neck** to be very much involved in something bad or illegal.

— **get it in the neck** to be severely scolded or punished.

— **have the brass neck to (do something)** to have the impertinence or brazenness to (do something).

— **neck and neck** exactly equal.

— **risk one's neck** to put one's life, job, etc, in danger.

— **stick one's neck out** to take a risk, to or do something that may cause trouble.

— **this *or* that, etc, neck of the woods** this or that, etc, part of the country.

NEED

— **the needful** money.

NEEDLE

— **like looking for a needle in a haystack** an impossible search.

NEGLECT

— **to be neglectful of**-accustomed to neglect or omit things.

NEITHER

— **neither fish (flesh) nor fowl**-(used to criticize something) not completely one thing or another; not in any one particular class.

— **neither here nor there**-not important.

NEVER

— **never-never land** an imaginary land where

conditions are ideal.
— **on the never-never** by hire purchase.

NEW
— **new broom** someone who has just been appointed to a post and who is eager to be efficient, make changes, etc.

NEWS
— **break the news to (someone)** to tell (someone) about something, usually something unpleasant or sad, that has happened.
— **no news is good news** if one has not received any information about someone or something then all is likely to be well since if something bad, such as an accident, had happened one would have heard.
— **that's news to me!** used to indicate one's lack of knowledge about a piece of information and often also one's surprise, annoyance, etc..

NEXT
— **next door to (something)** very nearly (something).
— **next to nothing** almost nothing, very little.
— **next to one's heart**-very near to one

NICK
— **in good** *or* **poor nick** in good or poor condition.
— **in the nick of time** just in time, at the last possible time.

NIGHT
— **be a night owl** to be in the habit of staying up late out of preference.

NINE
— **a nine days' wonder** something that arouses surprise and interest for a short time only.

NINEPINS
— **go down like ninepins** to become ill or damaged, or to be killed or destroyed rapidly, one after the other.

NIP

— **nip (something) in the bud** to put a stop or end to (something) as soon as it develops.

NONE

— **have/want none of it/that**-refuse to do; become involved in, accept or agree to something

— **none other than somebody**-used to emphasize who or what sb/ sth is, when this is surprising

— **none too cleaver, happy, quickly etc.**-not at all clever, quickly etc.

— **none too** not very.

NOSE

— **cut off one's nose to spite one's face** to do something that harms oneself, usually in order to harm someone else.

— **follow one's nose** to go straight forward.

— **get up (someone's) nose** to annoy or irritate (someone).

— **have a nose around** to have a good look round a place, usually out of curiosity and when one is not supposed to be doing so.

— **have a nose for (something)** to have a talent or ability for finding or noticing something.

— **keep (one's** *or* **someone's) nose to the grindstone** to keep (someone) working hard without stopping.

— **lead (someone) by the nose** to get (someone) to do whatever one wants.

— **look down one's nose at (someone** *or* **something)** to regard or treat (someone or something) with disdain or contempt.

— **nosey parker** someone who is too inquisitive about other people's affairs.

— **on the nose** exactly.

— **thumb one's nose at (someone** *or* **something)** *see* **thumb.**

— **turn up one's nose at (something)** to treat (something) with dislike or disgust.

— **under (someone's) (very) nose** (1) right in front of (someone) and so easily seen.

(2) while (someone) is actually present.

NOT

— **not a bit of it** (informal)-not in the least.
— **not a soul**-not a single person.
— **not be as/so black as he/she, etc. is painted**-not so bad as people say he/she, etc. is
— **not for the world**-not for anything.
— **not much cop** (informal)-not very good, not worth much.
— **not the only fish in the sea/pebble on the beach**-not the only suitable person.
— **not to mention, not to speak of**-and one might also mention, include, in addition.
— **not worth a rap** (informal)-of no value, worthless.

NOTE

— **of note** famous or important.
— **strike the right note** to say or do something suitable for the occasion.

NOTHING

— **come to nothing** to fail.
— **go for nothing** to be wasted or unsuccessful.
— **have nothing between the ears** *see* **ears.**
— **have nothing on (someone)** (1) not to be nearly as good, skilful, bad, etc, as (someone).
(2) to have no proof or evidence of (someone's) wrong doing.
— **have nothing to do with (someone** *or* **something)** to avoid contact with (someone or something).
— **nothing ventured, nothing gained** one cannot achieve anything if one does not make an attempt or take a risk.

NOW

— **as of now**-from now on; from this moment on.
— **every now and again/then**-occasionally.
— **nothing doing** (informal and impolite)-no, refuse.
— **nothing for it**-no choice; no alternative.
— **nothing like as good as** (informal)-not nearly as

good as; much worse than.

— **nothing more nor less than/nothing short of reality**-the same as above.

— **nothing succeeds like success**-one success leads to another.

— **nothing to write home about**-person or thing that is not very interesting or unusual.

NOWHERE

— **be in the middle of nowhere** be in a place which is a long way away from a town or city, a lot of people, etc, often carrying the suggestion that the place is boring.

— **get nowhere** to make no progress, to have no success.

— **nowhere near** not nearly.

NUCLEAR

— **go nuclear** to become extremely angry.

NUDGE

— **nudge, nudge, wink, wink** used to indicate that there is some form of sexual innuendo or hidden reference in something that has been said.

NULL

— **null and void (usually with reference to legal documents)**-not effective; having no force.

NUMBER

— **get** *or* **have (someone's) number** to find out or know what kind of person (someone) is and what he or she is likely to do.

— **(someone's) number is up** (someone) is about to suffer something unpleasant, such as dying, failing, being punished, being caught, etc.

— **number one** oneself.

NURSE

— **nurse a grudge**-neither forget nor forgive an injury that was done to one, keep active in one's mind a reason for not liking someone.

# O

---

OAK

— **great oaks from little acorns grow** a saying used to emphasize that even large and important things often begin a small way.

OAR

— **put** *or* **stick one's oar in** to interfere in another's affairs, conversation, e.g. by offering unwanted opinions.

— **rest on one's oars** to take a rest after working very hard.

OAT

— **off one's oats** not feeling well and so not eating much.

— **sow one's wild oats** *see* **wild.**

OATH

— **On/under oath-have** sworn to tell the truth in a court of law.

— **On my oath**-used to emphasize that one is telling the truth.

— **Swear/take an oath**-promise solemnly to tell the truth.

OBJECT

— **money, distance, etc, is no object** it does not matter how much money, distance, etc, is involved in the particular situation.

OCEAN

— **a drop in the ocean** *same as* **a drop in (he bucket** *see* **bucket.**

OFF

— **go off** to begin to dislike (someone or something previously liked).

— **in the offing** about to or likely to happen, appear, etc.
— **off and on** *or* **on and off** occasionally.

OFFENSIVE
— **Be on the offensive**-be making an attack.
— **Go on/take the offensive**-change one's tactic from defence to attack.

OFFEND
— **Offend against**-to do harm to, cause anger.

OIL
— **be no oil painting** to be not at all attractive.
— **oil and water** used to emphasize how different two people or things are.
— **oil the wheels** to make something easier to do or obtain.
— **pour oil on troubled waters** to attempt to bring a state of calm and peace to a situation of disagreement or dispute.
— **strike oil** to obtain exactly what one wants, to be successful.

OLD
— **an old hand** someone who is very experienced (at doing something).
— **old as the hills** extremely old.
— **old hat old**-fashioned, no longer popular.
— **old master** (a work by) any great painter before the 19th century, especially of the 15th and 16th centuries.
— **the old-boy (old-boy's) network** a system in which jobs and other advantages are obtained on the basis of knowing the right people rather than on ability or worth.
— **the old country** the country from which an immigrant or his or her parents or grandparents originally came.
— **the old guard** the older members of a group who are old-fashioned in their opinions and tastes.

ON
— **be not on** used to indicate emphatic disapproval

of or lack of acceptance of something.

— **be on to (someone)** having discovered some previously secret or unknown information about (someone) or his or her activities.
— **on an even keel**-in an orderly way to a well-organized, well-ordered state of affairs.
— **on a par/with equal to**-at the same level as.
— **on edge**-nervous; tense.
— **on end**-continuously, without a break.
— **on faith**-believing in something because one is told it is so.
— **on foot**-by walking.
— **on (one's) guard**-prepared against something, ready to defend oneself.
— **on hand**-available; ready to be used.
— **on one's hands**-in one's possession.
— **on one's shoulders**-part of one's responsibility.
— **on tenterhooks**-very tense, nervous.
— **on one's knees**-in a bad way; doing badly.
— **on no account**-for no reason whatsoever.
— **on the rails (informal)**-behaving normally, properly.
— **on the rocks**-ruined; finished.
— **on the ball (informal)**-very efficient; very good at what one does.
— **on in years**-old.
— **on one's own**-by oneself without help.
— **on one's own account**-for oneself personally.
— **on paper**-according to what has been written down.
— **on pins and needles**-in a very anxious or nervous state.
— **go on record**-state publicly.
— **on sale**-being sold

ONCE

— **give (someone) the once-over** to look at or study (someone or something) quickly.
— **once and for all** now and for the last time, finally.

ONE

— **a one-horse race** a competition, contest, etc, in which one person or side is certain to win.
— **a one-night stand** a relationship, arrangement, etc

that lasts for one evening or night only.

— **be at one with (someone)** to be in agreement with (someone).

— **be one up on (someone)** to have an advantage over (someone).

— **get one over on (someone)** to gain a victory or advantage over (someone).

— **have a one-track mind** to think only of one subject all the time.

– **have had one to many** to have had too much to drink.

– **it takes one to know one** used to indicate that people who have faults of their own find it easy to spot such faults I others.

— **not be oneself** to be feeling slightly unwell, to be more depressed, etc, than usual.

ONION

— **know one's onions** to know a subject, one's job, etc.

OPEN

— **an open-and-shut case** free from uncertainty, having an obvious outcome.

— **an open secret** a supposed secret that is known to many people.

— **keep an open mind** to be willing to listen to other people's suggestions, ideas, etc, instead of just concentrating on one's own point of view.

OPPOSITE

— **(someone's) opposite number** the person in another company, country, etc, whose job or role corresponds to someone's.

OPTION

— **keep one's options open** to delay making a definite decision so that all choices are available as long as possible.

ORACLE

— **work the oracle** to produce the desired result, to obtain what one wants, especially by using cunning, influence or bribery.

ORDER

— **out of order** (1) not working properly.
(2) not according to the conventions or rules of meetings, etc.

— **the order of the day** something that should be done, worn, etc, because conventional, common, fashionable, etc.

ORGAN

— **speak** to **the organ grinder, not his monkey** used to emphasize that one wants to deal with someone in authority, not with someone associated with him/her who has no power.

OTHER

— **look the other way** to ignore or disregard something wrong, illegal, etc.

— **or other** not known or decided.

OUT[1]

— **come out** to make public the fact that one is a homosexual.

— **out and about** going around outside, e.g. after an illness.

OUT[2]

— **out for (something)** wanting and trying to get (something).

— **out to (do something)** determined to (do something).

OVER

— **be all over (someone)** to be extremely friendly and attentive to (someone).

— **over and done with** completely finished, at an end.

OWN

— **come into one's own** to have the opportunity to show one's good qualities, talent, skill, etc.

— **hold one's own** (1) to perform as well as one's opponents in a contest, an argument, etc.
(2) to be surviving, to be holding on to life.

# P

P

— **mind one's p's and q's** to be very careful, to be polite and well-behaved.

PACE

— **keep pace with (someone *or* something)** to progress or develop at the same rate as (a person, subject or situation) with regard to social or financial standing, knowledge, etc.
— **put (someone *or* something) through its *or* his *or* her paces** to test the ability of (someone or something) by getting them to demonstrate what it, he or she is capable of.
— **set the pace for** to establish the rate at which, or the manner in which, an activity is carried out.
— **show one's paces** to demonstrate one's abilities.
— **stay the pace** to maintain progress in an activity at the same rate as others.

PACK

— **ahead of the pack** more successful than one's competitors or rivals.
— **pack it in** to stop doing something, e.g. working at something.
— **send (someone) packing** to send (someone) away firmly and frankly.

PACKET

— **make, lose, spend, etc. a packet**-make, etc. a large amount of money.

PART

— **for my, etc, part** as far as I, etc, am concerned.
— **look the part** to have the appropriate appearance

of a particular kind of person.

— **part and parcel (of something)** something that is naturally or basically part (of something).

— **take (something) in good part** to accept (something) without being angry or offended.

— **take (someone's) part** to support (someone) in an argument, debate, etc.

— **the parting of the ways** the point at which people must go different ways, take different courses of action, make different decisions, etc.

PARTIAL

— **partial to**-fond of

PARTING

— **parting of the ways**-going in different direction.

— **parting shot**-(often with reference to people who have been quarrelling) remark one makes and one is leaving

PARTY

— **bring (something) to the** party to make some kind of contribution to an activity, event, or situation.

— **(someone's) party piece** an act, joke, speech that someone frequently performs in public.

— **the life and soul of the party** *see* **life.**

— **the party line** the official opinions, ideas, attitudes, etc, asset down by the leaders of a particular group.

— **the party's over** a pleasant or happy time has come to an end.

PASS

— **let (something)** pass to choose to disregard (something).

— **make a pass at** (someone) to try to start a romantic or sexual relationship with (someone).

— **pass away** to die.

— **pass by on the other side to** ignore someone in trouble and not help him or her.

— **pass for (someone** *or* **something)** to be mistaken for (someone or something).

— **pass (something) up** not to accept (something).

PAST

— **I, etc, would not put it past (someone) to (do something)** I, etc, think (someone) is quite capable of (doing something bad).

— **past one's** *or* **its best** *or* **past it** less good, etc, than when one, or it, was not so old.

— **past master** someone extremely talented or skilful.

PASTURE

— **pastures new** *or* **fresh fields and pastures new** used to indicate a new and different place or situation.

PAT

— **a pat on the back** an indication of praise or approval.

PATCH

— **not to be a patch on (someone** *or* **something)** not to be nearly as good as (someone or something).

— **patch it** *or* **things up** to become friends again after a

PARROT

— **parrot-fashion** repeating words or ideas without understanding what they mean.

— **sick as a parrot** *see* **sick.**

PART

— **for my, etc, part** as far as I, etc, am concerned.

— **look the part** to have the appropriate appearance of a particular kind of person.

— **part and parcel (of something)** something that is naturally or basically part (of something).

— **take (something) in good part** to accept (something) without being angry or offended.

— **take (someone's) part** to support (someone) in an argument, debate, etc.

— **the parting of the ways** the point at which people must go different ways, take different courses of action, make different decisions, etc.

PARTY

— **bring (something) to the** party to make some kind

of contribution to an activity, event, or situation.
— **(someone's) party piece** an act, joke, speech that someone frequently performs in public.
— **the life and soul of the party** *see* **life.**
— **the party line** the official opinions, ideas, attitudes, etc, asset down by the leaders of a particular group.
— **the party's over** a pleasant or happy time has come to an end.

PASS
— **let (something)** pass to choose to disregard (something).
— **make a pass at** (someone) to try to start a romantic or sexual relationship with quarrel.

PATH
— **beat a path to (someone's) door** to visit (someone) very frequently or in large numbers.

PAVE
— **pave the way for (something)** to make it possible or easier for (something to happen).

PEOPLE
— **Of all people/places/things**-used to emphasize that the person/ place/thing is the most or least likely in the circumstances.
— **People who live in glass houses shouldn't throw stones**-you should not criticize other people for faults that you have yourself.

PERSON
— **in person**-with bodily presence; not through a deputy or representative by ones self

PERSPECTIVE
— **get put etc. something in/out of perspective**-be able/not be able to see or understand the relative importance of certain events, facts etc.

PERVERT
— **pervert the course of justice**-tell or lie or do something in order to prevent the police, etc. from

finding out the truth about a crime.

PETARD
— **hoist with one's own petard** to be the victim of one's own action which was intended to harm someone else.

PETER
— **to peter out**-to fail; to come to an end by degrees.

PICK
— **pick and choose** to choose very carefully from a range of things.

PICTURE
— **be out of the picture** to be no longer involved in something.
— **the big picture** the whole situation, not just some details.
— **get the picture** to understand what is being explained or described.
— **put (someone) in the picture** to give (someone) all the information and detail about a situation.

PIN
— **for two pins** given the least encouragement or reason.
— **on pins and needles** in a state of anxiety or suspense.
— **you could have heard a pin drop** there was silence.

PINCH
— **at a pinch** if it is absolutely necessary.
— **feel the pinch** to have financial problems.

PINE
— **to pine away**-to languish, to wear away through pain of body of distress to mind.
— **to pine for**-to grieve for, to be distressed for.

PLACE
— **fall into place** to become understood when seen in terms of its relationship to other things.

— **go places** to be successful in one's career.
— **in the first place** (1) in the beginning, to start with.
(2) as the first point in an argument, etc.
— **know one's place** to accept the lowliness of one's position and act accordingly.
— **a place in the sun** a situation in which one will be happy, successful, well of, etc..
— **pride of place** *see* **pride.**
— **put oneself in (someone's) place** to imagine what it would be like to be in (someone else's) circumstances.
— **put (someone) in his** *or* **her place** to remind (someone) angrily of the lowliness of his or her position or of his or her lack of experience, knowledge, etc.

PLAY
— **all work and no play makes Jack a dull boy** *see* **work.**
— **bring into play** to begin to use or employ.
— **child's play** *see* **child.**
— **fair play** *see* **fair.**
— **make a play for (someone** *or* **something)** to try to obtain (someone or something).
— **play (something) down** to try to make (something) appear less important, grave, etc.
— **played out** (1) exhausted.
(2) no longer having any interest, influence, usefulness, etc.
— **play fast and loose with (something)** *see* **fast.**

PLEDGE
— **To take or sign the pledge**-promise never to drink alcohol.

PLOT
— **the plot thickens** the situation is getting more complicated and more interesting.

PLOUGH
— **To put one's hand to the plough**-to commence serious work, to undertake important duties.
— **To plough the sands**-to do something unprofitable.

PLUCK
- **to pluck away**-to pull away.
- **to pluck off**-to tear off; to pull off with a jerk.
- **to pluck out**-to draw out suddenly; to tear out.
- **to pluck up one's courage or heart or spirits**-to regain confidence; to throw fear aside.

PLUG
- **pull the plug on** (something) to stop supporting (something), to stop (something) from continuing.

POCKET
- **in (someone's) pocket** under the control or influence of (someone).
- **line one's pocket** to make money for oneself dishonestly.
- **out of pocket** having made a loss.
- **to pick a person's pocket-to** steal from a person's pocket.
- **pocket one's pride-act** in a humble way because it is necessary.

POISON
- **hand/give (someone) a poisoned chalice** *see* **chalice.**
- **poison-pen letter** an anonymous letter saying bad things about someone.

POSSESSION
- **take possession of something**-become the owner of something.

POSSIBLE
- **as quickly, much soon etc. as possible**-as quickly, much, soon etc. as you can.

POSTAL
- **go postal**-become extremely angry or start behaving in a violent and angry way

POT
- **go to pot** to get into a bad or worse state.
- **keep the pot boiling** to keep something going or

operating.

— **take pot-luck** to have a meal at someone's house, etc, without having anything specially prepared for one.
— **the pot calling the kettle black** someone criticizing (someone) for doing (something) that he or she does himself or herself.
— **the** *or* **a watched pot** never boils when one is waiting for something to happen, etc, the time taken seems longer if one is constantly thinking about it.

POUND

— **pound of flesh**-something owed to someone which he/she demands in spite of the hardship which may come as a result.

PREMIUM

— **be at a premium** to be much in demand and, therefore, difficult to obtain.

PRETTY

— **come to a pretty pass** to get into a bad state.
— **cost a pretty penny** to cost a large amount of money.
— **sitting pretty** in a very comfortable or advantageous position.

PREY

— **be a prey to (something)** regularly to suffer from (something).
— **prey on (someone's) mind** to cause constant worry or anxiety to (someone).

PRICE

— **at a price** at a very high price.
— **a price on (someone's) head** a reward offered for the capture or killing of (someone).
— **what price (something)?** What do you think of (something)? What is the value of (something)?.

PRICK

— **kick against the pricks** to show opposition to those

in control or power.

PRIDE

— **pride goes before a fall** being too conceited often leads to misfortune.
— **pride of place** the most important or privileged position.
— **swallow one's pride** to behave in a more humble way than one usually does or than one would wish to do.

PROBS

— **No probs**-used to mean there is no problem.

PRODUCTION

— **make a production of (something)** to make (something) appear to be much more complicated than it actually is.

PROFILE

— **in profile**-(of a face) seen from the side.
— **adopt, keep etc. a high/ low profile**-try to/try not to attract other people's interest attention etc.

PULL

— **pull the other one!** used to emphasize to someone that you do not believe him or her.
— **pull through** to survive, to get better.

PULSE

— **keep one's finger on the pulse** to keep oneself informed about recent developments in a situation, organization, etc, or in the world.

PUMP

— **prime the pump** to take some kind of action to help something happen or succeed, often by contributing money.

PUT

— **put/turn back the clock**-do things in an old-fashioned way.
— **put one's foot down**-be firm; insist that what one

wants to be done is carried out

— **put our/their/your heads together**-consult together, share one another's ideas

— **put/set one's (own) house in order**-arrange one's affairs properly

— **put the anchors on** (informal)-brake; suddenly slow down.

— **put the arm/the screws on someone** (informal)-try to force someone to do something

— **put on a bold/brave front/face**-pretend to be calm, not worried

— **put on an act/a big act**-pretend to be something that one is not, e.g., frightened, injured, etc.

— **put it to someone**-suggest to someone (often used by lawyers taking to witnesses, etc.)

— **put/shove/stick one's oar in** (informal)-give opinions or suggestions without being asked for them

— **put out feelers/a feeler**-try to find out something in a careful way.

— **put (someone) out of the way**-kill, get rid of someone.

— **put out the welcome mat**-make someone feel welcome.

— **be put upon** to be made use of for someone else's benefit, to be taken advantage of.

# Q

QUAKING

— **(be) Quaking/shaking in your boots/shoes**-be very worried or frightened.

QUALIFY

— **To qualify for**-to render or become capable of.

QUANDARY

— **To be in the quandary**-to be in difficulty, to be in hard plight.

QUANTITY

— **an unknown quantity** someone or something of which very little is known.

QUARREL

— **to quarrel over**-to dispute about a thing or matter.
— **to quarrel with**-to have a dispute with someone.
— **the quarrel with one's bread and butter**-to do something which may result in depriving one of the means of his livelihood.

QUARTERS

— **at close quarters** nearby, at or from a short distance away.

QUEEN

— **Queen it**-behave as if in a position of power.
— **Queen of grace**-virgin Mary.

QUEER

— **a queer fish** *see* **fish.**
— **in Queer Street** in financial difficulties.
— **queer (someone's) pitch** to upset (someone's) plans or arrangements.

QUESTION

— **a loaded question** *see* **load.**

— **a question mark over (something)** doubt or uncertainty in relation to (something).

— **out of the question** not possible.

— **pop the question** to ask (someone) to marry one.

— **rhetorical question** *see* **rhetorical.**

— **the sixty-four (thousand) dollar question** *see* **sixty.**

QUEUE

— **jump the queue** to go ahead of others in a queue without waiting for one's proper turn.

QUIET

— **keep quiet about something; keep something quiet**-say nothing about something; keep the secret.

— **on the quiet**-without telling anyone; secretly.

— **as quiet as a mouse**-(of a person) saying very little or making very little noise.

QUITE

— **quite something** something special or remarkable.

— **quite so**-(rather old-fashioned) I agree.

— **not quiet the thing**-not considered socially acceptable.

— **quite the best, the worst, etc. something**-absolutely the best, worst etc.

— **quite some time**-quite a long time.

QUIT

— **call it quits** to agree that neither person owes the other one anything and that neither one has any kind of advantage over the other.

# R

RABBIT

— **rabbit on (about somebody/something)**-to talk continuously usually about things that are not important or interesting.

RACK[1]

— **go to rack and ruin** to fall into a state of disrepair or into a worthless condition.

RACK[2]

— **on the rack** in distress, under strain.

RACKET

— **To be on the racket**-to spend one's time in pleasure, frolic or dissipation.

RAG

— **lose one's rag** to lose one's temper.
— **run (someone) ragged** to cause (someone) to be exhausted.

RAGE

— **all the rage** very fashionable or popular.
— **from rage to riches**-from being very poor to being very rich especially in a short period of time

RAID

— **to raid the market**-to bring down prices by creating panic.

RAIL

— **jump the rails** suddenly to go wrong.
— **off the rails** not sensible, disorganized, deranged.

RAIN

— **keep** *or* **put away** *or* **save (something) for a rainy day** to keep (something, especially money) until one really needs it.
— **right as rain** perfectly all right, completely well.
— **rain on (someone's) parade** to spoil (someone's) plans or special occasion.
— **rain or shine** whatever the weather.
— **rain like cats and dogs** *see* **cat.**
— **take a rain check on (something)** used to indicate that you are unable to accept an invitation but would like to postpone it until a later date.

RAINY

— **(for a) rainy hell**-make it clear that one is angry.

RAISE

— **raise eyebrows**-cause people to be shocked or surprised.
— **raise the roof**-make a very loud noise (by applause, cheering, etc.)
— **to raise one's back**-to rebel, to grow obstinate.
— **to raise money on**-to get money by mortgaging something.

RAKE

— **thin as a rake** extremely thin.
— **to rake up**-to revive
— **rake around for/something**-to search carefully

RAM

— **ram (something) down (someone's) throat** *see* **throat.**

RAMP

— **on the ramp**-in state of excitement, wild

RAMPAGE

— **be** *or* **go on the rampage** to rush about wildly or violently.

RANDOM

— **at random**-haphazard, aimlessly

RANK

— **close ranks** to act together and support each other as a defensive measure.
— **pull rank** to make unfair use of a position of authority to make someone else do as one wishes or to give one some kind of advantage.
— **the rank and file** the ordinary people or the ordinary members of an organization, etc.

RANSOM

— **hold (someone) to ransom** to demand something (from someone) by threatening to take harmful action if it is not given.

RANT

— **rant and rave** to shout angrily.

RATHER

— **rather better than**-somewhat in excess of

REACH

— **reach for the stars**-try to be successful at something that is difficult.
— **within (easy) reach (of something)**-close to something.

READ

— **take (something) as read** to assume (something).
— **read between the lines**-see a meaning which is suggested but not openly stated
— **read someone like a book**-be able to know what someone is thinking or planning
— **read someone's mind**-know what someone is thinking.
— **read (someone) the Riot Act**-speak angrily (to someone) because he/she has done something wrong

READY

— **ready money**-money which can be immediately made use of, cash.
— **ready witted**-clear, sharp
— **to make ready**-to prepare

REASON
— **it stands to reason that** it is logical, or obvious that.
— **ours, etc, not to reason why** it is not for us, etc, to question orders.
— **see reason** to be persuaded by someone's advice, etc, to act or think sensibly.
— **within reason** within sensible limits.
— **without rhyme or reason** *see* **rhyme.**

REBEL
— **to rebel against**-to oppose the lawful authority, to revolt.

REBOUND
— **on the rebound** while suffering from the disappointment of the end of a relationship.

RECEDE
— **to recede from**-to retreat or withdraw from.

RECKON
— **to reckon for**-to be answerable for
— **to reckon with**-to settle accounts or claim, to deal with
— **to reckon on (or upon)-to** count or depend upon.

RECOVER
— **to recover from**-to bring back to former state.

RED
— **a red-letter day** a day remembered because something particularly pleasant or important happened or happens on it.
— **bleed red ink** *see* **ink.**
— **catch (someone) red-handed** to find (someone) in the act of doing something wrong or unlawful.
— **in the red** in debt, overdrawn.
— **like a red rag to a bull** certain to make (someone) *angy.*
— **on red alert** ready for an an immediate danger.
— **paint the town red** *see* **paint.**
— **red-hot** very enthusiastic or dedicated.
— **red tape** the rules and regulations official papers,

etc, that are thought to characterize government departments.
— **see red** to get very angry.

REDOUND
— **redound to one's credit (formal)**-cause one to be praised.

REDUCE
— **to reduce to**-to bring down to
— **reduce someone to tears**-make someone cry, weep.

RESPOND
— **to respond to**-to reply to, to answer to.

REST
— **come to rest** to stop.
— **give it a rest** used to tell someone to stop going on and on talking about a subject that is annoying or boring.
— **lay (someone) to rest** to bury(someone).
— **rest assured** you can be quite certain.

RETURN
— **return to the fold** to come back to one's family, an organization, a set of principles or beliefs, etc, which one has previously left.

RIDE
— **be riding for a fall** to be on a course of action that is likely to lead to unpleasant results or disaster for oneself.
— **go along for the ride** to do something that other people are doing just for enjoyment or interest, not because one is seriously involved in it.
— **have a rough ride** to receive harsh treatment or suffer an unpleasant experience.
— **ride out (something)** to survive until (something difficult) is over.
— **take (someone) for a ride** to deceive or trick (someone).

RIGHT
— **by rights** rightly, justly.

— **(someone's) left hand does not know what his** *or* **her right one** is **doing** *see* **left.**
— **Mr** *or* **Miss Right** the perfect man or woman for one to marry.
— **not right in the head** deranged, insane, mentally handicapped.
— **put (something) right** to repair, to make all right, to rectify.

RISE
— **rise and shine** to get out of bed and be lively and cheerful.
— **take a rise out of (someone)** to tease or make fun of (someone) so that he or she gets annoyed.

RISK
— **run the risk of (something** *or* **doing something)** to do (something) that involves a risk of (something or doing something).

ROCKET
— **not rocket science** used to indicate that something is quite easy and does not require much intellect or skill.

ROLL
— **a rolling stone (gathers no moss)** a person who does not stay very long in one place (does not acquire very much in the way of possessions or responsibilities).
— **be rolling in it** *or* **in money** to have a great deal of money.
— **be rolling in the aisles** to be laughing very heartily.
— **roll on** may (a particular time) come soon.

ROSE
— **come up smelling of roses** to come out of a situation with some kind of advantage when it was expected to result in blame or harm for
— **everything's coming up roses** everything is turning out to be successful or happy.
— **look at (someone** *or* **something) through rose-coloured** *or* **rose-tinted spectacles** *or* **glasses** to

view (someone or something) in an extremely optimistic light.

ROUGH
— **cut up rough** to get very nasty.
— **give (someone) the rough edge of one's tongue** to scold or criticize (someone) severely.
— **have some/a few rough edges** *see* **edge.**
— **live rough** to live without proper housing, often outside all the time, and without the usual amenities.
— **ride roughshod over (someone)** to treat (someone) without any respect and without any regard for his or her views or feelings.
— **take the rough with the smooth** to accept the disadvantages as well as the advantages and benefits of a situation.

ROUND
— **get round to (something)** to find time and opportunity to do (something), to do something when one can.
— **go the rounds** to be passed from person to person.
— **in round figures** *or* **numbers** to the nearest whole number, especially one that can be divided by ten.
— **round trip** the journey to somewhere plus the journey back.

RULE
— **rule of thumb** a rough or inexact guide used for calculations of some kind.

RUN
— **a run for (someone's) money** a creditable or worthy performance or opposition.
— **(someone's) cup runneth** over someone feels very happy.
— **in the running** with a chance of success.
— **make the running** to be the leader, to set the pace, fashion or standard.
— **on the run** running away.
— **run across (someone** *or* **something)** to meet or find (someone or something) by chance.
— **run its course** to continue to its natural end, to develop naturally.

# S

SABRE

— **rattle one's sabre** to put on a show of anger or fierceness without resorting to physical force in order to frighten someone.

SACK

— **get the sack** to be dismissed from one's job.

— **sackcloth and ashes** sorrow or apology for what one has done or failed to do.

SAID

— **enough said**-used to say that you understand a situation and there is no need to say any more.

— **the less/least said, the better**-it is better in a difficult situation to say nothing or very little.

— **when all is said and done**-when ail the facts are considered.

SAME

— **be all the same to (someone)** to be a matter of no importance to (someone).

SCARE

— **scare (someone) stiff** make (someone) very frightened.

SCHOOL

— **of the old school** believing in or practising customs, codes of behaviour, ideas, etc, no longer popular.

SEAL

— **set one's** *or* **the seal (of approval) on (something)** to give one's agreement or approval to (something).

SEE
— **see red**-be extremely angry.
— **see someone (all) right** (informal)-look after someone, make sure that someone gets what he needs.
— **see stars**-be in a dazed condition, *e.g.*, after bumping one's head.
— **see the color of someone's money** (informal)-see that someone actually has the necessary cash with him.
— **see the red light**-stop doing something because one realizes that it is harmful or dangerous
— **to see about (or to) a thing**-to look after or attend to something.
— **to see off**-to accompany to a place of departure.
— **to see double**-to be drunk.
— **to see the light**-to be revealed or discovered.
-- **to see through**-to discern, to watch to the end to help.
— **to see how the wind blows**-to observe if the circumstances are favorable or adverse.
— **see at the world through rose-colored/rosetinted/ rosy glasses/ spectacles-have** a cheerful attitude to life in general, not paying any attention to the unpleasant side of things.
— **see to** it-make sure that something is done.

SENSE
— **come to one's senses** to begin to behave or think sensibly.
— **take leave of one's senses** to become deranged or very foolish.

SEPARATE
— **separate/tell the sheep from the gooats**-make a distinction between those who are good, intelligent, suuccessful, etc. and those who are not.

SERIOUSLY
— Take somebody/something seriously-consider or treat something as important or serious.

SERVE
— **serve/fulfill its/one's/the purposes**-do what it/one

is required to do.

— **serve no purpose**-be useless.

— **serve someone right**-(the word serve can either be used in an unchanging way or as a normal verb) be a punishment that someone deserves.

— **to serve a sentence**-to undergo entire period of prescribed punishment

— **to serve one out**-to take revenge on one.

— **to serve the purpose of**-to be enough for, to be adequate for

— **to serve the turn**-suffice for one's need, to suit one's purpose.

— **to serve up**-to bring to table, to present food to eat.

— **to serve one a trick**-to play a trick on one.

— **to serve one right**-to treat one as he deserves.

The judge served him right by imposing a heavy find for the crime of adulteration.

SERVICE

— **at (someone's) service** ready to be of assistance to (someone).

— **have seen good service** to have been well used and reliable.

SET

— **set an example**-behave well, do something well, so that others can copy or imitate

— **set someone/something at rest**-clam someone/something down

— **set one's face against-be** opposed to

— **set forth**-describe, explain

— **set one's heart/mind on**-want (to do) something very much

— **to set aside**-to disregard, to annul

— **to set about**-to begin

— **to set in order**-to adjust, to arrange

— **to set at ease**-to quieten, to contain, to rest

— **to set one's face**-to turn oneself resolutely towards

SHELL
— **come out of one's shell** to become less shy.

SHINE
— **take a shine to (someone)** to become fond of (someone).

SHORT
— **by a short head** by a very small amount.
— **caught** *or* **taken short** having a sudden, urgent need to go to the toilet.
— **give (someone** *or* **something) short shrift** to spend very little time or thought on (someone or something).
— **go short** not to have or take enough of something that one needs.
— **make short work of (something)** to deal with or get rid of (something) very quickly.
— **run short of (something)** to begin not to have enough of (something).
— **sell (someone** *or* **something) short** not to do justice to, to belittle (someone or something).

SHOT
— **a long shot** a guess or attempt unlikely to be accurate or successful, but worth trying.
— **a shot across the bows** something given as a warning.
— **a shot in the arm** something that helps to revive (something).
— **big shot** an important person.
— **call the shots** to be in charge of events or a situation.
— **like a shot** very quickly or willingly.
— **shotgun wedding** a forced wedding, usually because the bride is pregnant.

SHOULDER
— **a shoulder to cry on** a sympathetic listener.
— **put one's shoulder to the wheel** to begin to work hard.
— **rub shoulders with (someone)** to associate closely with (someone).
— **shoulder to shoulder** side by side.

SHOW
— **a show of hands** a vote expressed by people raising their hands.
— **for show** for appearance, in order to impress people.
— **get the show on the road** to get something started or put into operation.
— **run the show** to be in charge of an organisation, etc.
— **show off** to behave in such a way as to impress others with one's possessions, ability, etc.
— **steal the show** to attract the most attention at an event.

SIDE
— **let the side down** to hinder one's colleagues by not performing, etc, as well as they have.
— **on the side** in a way other than by means of one's ordinary occupation.
— **side by side** beside one another.
— **take sides** to support a particular person, group, etc, against another.

SIEVE
— **have a memory like a sieve** to be extremely forgetful.

SIT
— **sit (something) out** to do nothing and simply wait for the end of (something) unpleasant.

SIX
— **a sixth sense** intuition, an ability to feel or realize something not perceived by the five senses.
— **at sixes and sevens** in a state of confusion and chaos.
— **knock (someone) for six** to take (someone) completely by surprise.
— **six of one and half a dozen of another** so similar as to make no difference.

SIXTY
— **the sixty-four (thousand) dollar question** the most important and/or difficult question.

SIZE
— **cut (someone) down to size** to humble (someone), to reduce (someone's) sense of his or her own importance.
— **size up (someone** *or* **something)** to consider carefully and form an opinion of the worth, nature, etc, of (someone or something).

SMALL
— **it's a small world** an expression used when one meets someone one knows somewhere unexpected.
— **make (someone) look small** to make (someone) seem foolish or insignificant.
— **small talk** light conversation about trivial matters.
— **small wonder** it is not at all surprising.
— **the small print** the parts of a document where important information is given without being easily noticed.

SMART
— **a smart Alec** someone who thinks he or she is very clever.
— **look smart** to be quick.

SOAP
— **soap opera** a radio or television serial broadcast regularly and dealing with the daily lives, problems, etc, of the characters.

SOON
— **no sooner said than done** a request will be fulfilled as soon as it is made.
— **speak too soon** to say something that takes for granted something not yet accomplished.

SPARE
— **a square peg in a round hole** *see* **peg.**
— **go spare** to become very angry or distressed.
— **spare tyre** a roll of fat round the middle of the body.

SPEAK
— **be on speaking terms** to be friendly towards

someone and communicate with him or her.
— **speak for itself** to need no explanation.
— **to speak of** worth mentioning.

SPIRIT
— **spirit (someone *or* something) away** to carry away (someone or something) secretly and suddenly.
— **the spirit is willing (but the flesh is weak)** one is not always physically able to do the things that one wishes do.

STAND
— **know where one stands** to know the exact nature of one's position or situation.
— **make a stand against (something)** to oppose or resist (something one believes to be wrong etc).
— **not to stand an earthly** *same as* **not to have an earthly** *see* **earthly.**
— **stand by** (1) to provide help and support for (someone).
(2) to be ready to take action.
— **stand corrected** to accept that one has been wrong.
— **stand one's ground** *see* **ground.**
— **stand in for (someone)** to act as a substitute for (someone).
— **stand on ceremony** to be very formal.
— **stand out for (something)** to go on protesting or resisting until one gets (something).
— **stand (someone) up** not to keep a promise to meet (someone).
— **stand up and be counted** to declare one's opinions publicly.
— **stand up for (someone)** to support or defend (someone).
— **stand up to (someone)** to face (someone) boldly, to show resistance to (someone).

STEP
— **step by step** gradually.
— **step in** to intervene.
— **step on it** to hurry.

— **step (something) up** to increase (something).
— **take steps** to take action of some kind.

STICK
— **a stick to beat (someone) with** something which can be used to criticize or damage (someone).
— **be on a sticky wicket** to **be** in a difficult or awkward situation that is difficult to defend.
— **come to a sticky end** to meet some misfortune or an unpleasant death.
— **get hold of the wrong end of the stick** to misunderstand a situation or something said or done.

STOP
— **pull out all the stops** to put as much effort and energy into something as possible.
— **stop at nothing** to be willing to do absolutely anything, however wrong, etc.
— **stop dead** to stop suddenly and abruptly.
— **stop over** to stay overnight somewhere while on a journey.
— **stop short of (something *or* doing something)** not to go as far as (something or doing something).

STRAW
— **a straw in the wind** a small or minor incident, etc, that indicates what may happen in the future.
— **clutch at straws** to hope that something may happen to get one out of a difficulty or danger when this is extremely unlikely.
— **draw the short straw** to be the one in a group who has to perform an unpleasant or undesirable task.

STRIDE
— **get into one's stride** to become accustomed to doing something and so do it well and effectively.
— **make great strides** to make very good progress.
— **take (something) in one's stride** to cope with (something) without worrying about it.

# T

TAB

— **keep tabs on (someone *or* something)** to keep a check on (someone or something).
— **pick up the tab for (something)** to pay for (something).

TABLE

— **turn the tables on (someone)** to change a situation so that one gains the advantage (over someone) after having been at a disadvantage.

TAIL

— **be on (someone's) tail** to be following someone closely.
— **chase one's tail** to spend a great deal of time and effort trying to do something but achieving very little.
— **have one's tail up** to be confident of success.
— **the tail is wagging the dog** used to indicate that a small or unimportant part of something is being allowed to control the whole thing.
— **turn tail** to turn round and leave a difficult or dangerous situation.
— **with one's tail between one's legs** in an ashamed, miserable or defeated state.

TAKE

— **be taken with (someone *or* something)** to find (someone or something) attractive.
— **take after (someone)** to resemble.
— **take (someone) in** to deceive (someone).
— **take it out on (someone)** to treat (someone) in an angry or nasty way because one is disappointed, angry, etc, about something.
— **take off** suddenly to become successful.

— **take (someone) off** to mimic (someone).

TALK

— **talk about (something)!** that is a good example of (something).

— **talk down to (someone)** to speak to (someone) in a condescending way as if he or she were inferior.

— **talk nineteen to the dozen** to talk a great deal and usually very rapidly.

TASTE

— **leave a nasty taste in the mouth** to leave someone with unpleasant memories or associations.

— **a taste of one's own medicine** *same as* **a dose of one's own medicine**-*see* **dose.**

TELL

— **I told you so I** warned you and I was right to do so.

— **there's no telling** it is impossible to know.

— **you never can tell** it is possible.

— **you're telling me!** that is definitely the case.

THANK

— **have only oneself to thank for (something)** to be the cause of (one's own misfortune).

THAT

— **just like that** immediately, without further consideration, discussion, etc.

— **that's that** there is no more to be said or done.

THICK

— **a bit thick** more than can be tolerated.

— **give (someone) a thick ear** to slap (someone) across the ear, to box (someone's) ears.

— **thick and fast** in great quantities and at a fast rate.

— **thick as thieves** extremely friendly.

— **thick as two short planks** extremely stupid.

— **through thick and thin** what ever difficulties arise.

THIN
— **be thin on top** to be balding.
— **have a thin time of it** to have an unpleasant or difficult time, especially because of money difficulties.

THING
— **do one's (own) thing** to do what one likes to do or what one is good at doing.
— **not to know the first thing about (something)** *see* **first.**
— **see things** to see someone or something that is not there.
— **the thing is** the most important point or question is.

THINK
— **have another think coming** to be quite mistaken.
— **not to think much of (someone** *or* **something)** to have a low opinion of (someone or something).

THUMB
— **thumb a lift** to ask for (and get) a lift in someone's vehicle by signalling with one's thumb.
— **thumb one's nose at (someone or something)** to express defiance or contempt at (someone or something), originally by making the rude gesture of putting one's thumb to one's nose.
— **thumbs down** rejection or disapproval.
— **thumbs up** acceptance or approval.
— **twiddle one's thumbs** to do nothing, to be idle.
— **under (someone's) thumb** under one's control or domination.

TIME
— **ahead of one's time** with ideas in advance of one's contemporaries, often not understood.
— **all in good time** soon, when it is the right time.
— **at one time** at a time in the past.
— **behind the times** not up-to-date, old-fashioned.
— **do time** to be in prison.
— **half the time** for a good part of the time, frequently.
— **have a time of it** to have a difficult time.
— **have no time for (someone** *or* **something)** to have a

very low opinion of (someone or something) and to wish not to associate with him or her or it.
— **have the time of one's life** to have a very enjoyable time.
— **have time on one's hands** to have more free time than one can usefully fill with work, etc.
— **in good time** early enough, with time to spare.
— **in (someone's) own good time** when it is convenient for (someone), at whatever time or speed he or she chooses.
— **kill time** to find something to do to pass some idle time, especially time spent waiting for someone or something.
— **make good time** to have as rapid, or more rapid, a journey as one expected.
— **mark time** to remain in one's present position without progressing or taking any action.
— **not before time** not too soon, rather late.
— **no time at all** a very short time.
— **on time** at the right time.
— **pass the time of day with (someone)** to greet (someone) and have a brief conversation, e.g. about the weather.
— **play for time** to act so as to delay an action, event, etc, until the time that conditions are better for oneself.
— **take one's time** not to hurry, to take as much time as wishes to do something.

TOP[1]
— **blow one's top** to lose one's temper.
— **get on top of one** used to indicate that someone is not coping with all the things that require to be done.
— **off the top of one's head** without much thought, without research or preparation.
— **the top of the ladder** *or* **tree** the highest point in a profession, etc.

TOP[2]
— **sleep like a top** to sleep very soundly.

TOUCH
— **a soft touch** *see* **soft**.

— **in touch with (someone)** in communication with (someone).
— **it's touch and go** it's very uncertain or precarious.
— **kick (something) into touch** to reject (something) or avoid dealing with it.
— **lose one's touch** to lose one's usual skill or knack.

TRIAL
— **trial and error** the trying out of various approaches or methods of doing something until one finds the right one.
— **trials and tribulations** difficulties and hardships.

TRY
— **try it on** to act in a bold way in order to find out to what extent it will be tolerated.

TURN
— **a turn-up for the books** something favourable which happens unexpectedly.
— **do (someone) a good turn** to help (someone) in some way.
— **do a U-turn** *see* **U.**
— **done to a turn** cooked exactly right, cooked to perfection.
— **turn of phrase** a way of expressing something.
— **turn (someone) off** to arouse feelings of dislike, disgust, etc in (someone).

TWICE
— **think twice** to give careful consideration.

TWO
— **put two and two together** to come to a (correct) conclusion from what one sees and hears.

# U

UP
— **be on the up-and-up** to be making successful progress.
— **be (well) up in** *or* **on (something)** to have an extensive knowledge of (something).
— **be up and running** to have started and be operating well.
— **be up with (someone)** to be wrong with (someone).
— **up and about** out of bed, after an illness.
— **up-and-coming** likely to be successful, rising in popularity or prominence.
— **up and doing** active and busy.
— **ups and downs** good fortune and bad fortune, successful periods and unsuccessful periods.
— **upstage (someone** *or* **something)** to take attention or interest away from (someone or something).

UPSHOT
— **the upshot** the result or outcome.

UPPER
— **have** *or* **get the upper hand (of** or **over) (someone)** have or get an advantage or control (over someone).
— **on one's uppers** very poor.
— **upper-crust** of the upper class or aristocracy.

UPSIDE
— **be** *or* **get upsides with (someone)** to be or become on a level with or equal with (someone).
— **turn (something) upside down** to put (something) into a state of disorder and confusion.

USE
— **come in useful** to be useful in the future.

# V

VAIN

— **take (someone's) name in vain** to use (someone's) name disrespectfully, especially to swear using God's name.

VARIETY

— **variety is the spice of life** the opportunity to do different things, experience different situations, etc, is what makes life interesting.

VEIL

— **draw a veil over (something)** not to discuss (something), to keep (something) hidden or secret.

VENGEANCE

— **with a vengeance** very strongly, much, etc.

VERY

— **the very thing** exactly what is required.

VEX

— **a vexed question** a difficult issue or problem that is much discussed without being resolved.

VICTORY

— **landslide victory** a victory in an election by a very large number of votes.

VIEW

— **a bird's-eye view of (something)** (1) a view of (something) seen from high above.
(2) a brief description, etc, of (something).

— **in view of (something)** considering (something), because of (something).

VILLAIN

— **the villain of the piece** the person responsible for an act of evil or wrongdoing.

VINE

— **a clinging vine** a possessive person, someone who likes always to be with someone else.

— **wither on the vine** to die to come to an end without being used, finished, etc.

VIOLET

— **a shrinking violet** a very timid, shy person.

VIPER

— **nurse a viper in one's bosom** to be helpful to, or supportive of, someone who does one harm.

VITAL

— **vital statistics** one's chest, waist and hip measurements.

VOICE

— **a voice crying in the wilderness** (someone) expressing an opinion or warning that no one takes any notice of.

— **the still, small voice (of reason)** the expression of a calm, sensible point of view.

VOLUME

— **speak volumes** to express a great deal of meaning without putting it into words.

VOTE

— **a vote of confidence** a vote taken to establish whether or not the government, a group of people, a person, etc, is still trusted and supported.

— **like turkeys voting for Christmas** *see* **turkey.**

— **vote with one's feet** to leave.

The workers had no confidence in the new management and so they voted with their feet by finding other jobs.

# W

WAGON

— **circle the wagons** of a group of people, to work together to protect themselves against possible harm or danger.

— **fall off the wagon** to start drinking again after having stopped.

— **hitch one's wagon to a star** to have noble or high ambitions or aims.

— **on the wagon** not drinking alcohol.

WAIT

— **lie in wait** to be on the watch (for someone), to ambush (someone).

WAKE

— **a wake-up call** something that rouses or shocks people into taking action.

— **in the wake of (something)** immediately following, and often caused by (something).

WALK

— **walk it** to win or succeed easily.

— **walk of life** occupation or profession, way of earning a living.

WALL

— **be climbing the wall(s)** to feel frustrated, bored or impatient.

— **go to the wall** to suffer ruin.

— **hit the wall** to reach a point where you can go no further or achieve any more.

— **nail (someone) to the wall** to punish someone severely or make him/her suffer because one is very angry.

— **off the wall** unconventional, strange.
— **up the wall** very annoyed, irritated, harassed, etc.
— **walls have ears** someone may be listening (to a secret conversation.

WALTER
— **a Walter Mitty** someone who invents stories about himself to make his life seem more exciting.

WAR
— **have been in the wars** to have a slight injury.
— **on the warpath** very angry.
— **a war of words** a fierce argument or disagreement.

WART
— **warts and all** including all the faults, disadvantages.

WASH
— **come out in the wash** to come to a satisfactory end.
— **washed-out** exhausted.
— **washed-up** ruined, finished.
— **(something) won't wash** to be regarded as unacceptable or incredible.

WASTE
— **be a waste of space** to be completely useless.
— **blow (someone** or **something) out of the water** to destroy or defeat (someone or something) utterly.
— **lay waste (something)** to destroy or ruin (something) by force.
— **waste not, want not** if one is careful not to waste anything it is likely that one will never be in want.

WATER
— **hold water** to be accurate, to be able to be proved true.
— **muddy the waters** to confuse a situation.
— **test the water/waters** to try to find out what the reaction is likely to be to a plan before one puts this into effect.

— **tread water** to take very little action.
— **water (something) down** to make (something) less serious, exciting, etc, than it really was.
— **water under the bridge** something that is past and cannot be changed and should be forgotten.

WATERFRONT
— **cover the waterfront** to cover a wide range of things or a wide range of aspects of something.

WAVE
— **make waves** to cause trouble.
— **on the same wavelength as (someone)** having the same opinions, attitudes, tastes, etc, as (someone).

WAY
— **be set in one's ways** to have a set routine in your life and to dislike having this disrupted.
— **get into the way of (something *or* doing something)** to become accustomed to (something or doing something).
— **get *or* have one's own way** to do or get what one wants.
— **go back a long way** used to indicate that people have known each other for a long time.
— **go out of one's way** to do more than is really necessary, to make a special effort.
— **go the way of all flesh** to die or come to an end.
— **have a way with (someone *or* something)** to have a special knack with (someone or something), to be good at handling (someone or something).
— **have come a long way** to have changed or improved a great deal since starting out.
— **have everything one's own way** to get everything done according to one's wishes.
— **have it both ways** to have the advantages of two sets of situations, each of which usually excludes the possibility of the other.
— **in a bad way** very ill, injured, distressed, etc.
— **lead the way** to go first, to be in front.
— **lose one's way** to cease to know where one is or which direction one is going in.

— **make one's way** to go, to progress.
— **make way for (someone** *or* **something)** to stand aside to leave room for (someone or something).
— **mend one's ways** to improve one's behaviour.
— **not to know which way to turn** to be in trouble and to be too confused to be able to decide what to do for the best.
— **one way and another** in various ways.
— **on the way** about to happen or arrive.
— **pay one's way** to pay one's expenses or one's share of expenses.
— **see one's way to (doing something)** to be able and willing to (do something).
— **there are no two ways about it** no other opinion, attitude, etc, is possible.
— **under way** in progress.
— **ways and means** methods, especially unofficial ones.
— **where's there's a will there's a way** a saying used to indicate that if one is determined to do something, then one will find a way to succeed in doing so.

WAYSIDE
— **fall by the wayside** to fail to continue to the end of something; to give up in the course of doing something.

WEAK
— **in a weak moment** at a time when one is feeling unusually kind, generous, sympathetic, etc.

WEAR
— **be the worse for wear** (1) to be in a bad state, looking tired, ill, untidy, etc.
(2) to be drunk.

WEATHER
— **under the weather** unwell:

WEB
— **a tangled web** used to describe a very complicate,

confused situation.

WEDGE
— **drive a wedge between** to cause disagreement or ill will between two people or two groups, especially when they were formerly friendly.
— **the thin end of the wedge** a minor event or action which could be the first stage of something major and serious or harmful.

WEIGHT
— **a weight off one's mind** used to indicate that one no longer has to worry about something which has been worrying one for some time.
— **carry weight** to have influence, to be considered important.
— **pull one's weight** to do one's fair share of work, etc.
— **punch above one's weight** to try to do something which is thought to be beyond one's abilities.
— **take the weight off one's feet** to sit down.
— **throw one's weight about** *or* **around** to use one's power and influence in a bullying way.
— **throw one's weight behind (someone** or **something)** to support (someone or something).
— **weigh (something) up** to assess (something).

WELL
— **be well out of (something)** to be fortunate in having got out of (something).

WELLY
— **give it some welly** to put effort and energy into doing something.
— **well off** (1) having plenty of money, rich.
(2) in a fortunate situation.

WEST
— **go west** to be ruined, to be finished.

WET
— **wet behind the ears** to be young, inexperienced and naive.

WHALE

— **have a whale of a time** to have an extremely enjoyable time.

WHAT

— **give (someone) what for** to scold or punish (someone).

— **know what's what** to know the details of a situation, to know what is going on.

— **what have you** and similar things.

— **what of it?** what does it matter?.

WHEEL

— **a fifth wheel** a person or thing that is not needed or is not wanted.

— **keep the wheels turning** to keep (something) operating smoothly.

— **reinvent the wheel** to do something which one considers new or innovative, but which is, in fact, very similar to something which has been done by someone else; to start a project from scratch without taking advantage of available information, research, etc.

— **wheeling and dealing** acting in an astute but sometimes dishonest or immoral way, especially in business.

— **wheels within wheels** used to indicate a very complicated situation with many different things involved, all influencing each other.

WHILE

— **worth (someone's) while** worth (someone's) time and effort.

WHIP

— **have the whip hand** to have control or an advantage..

— **a whipping boy** someone who is blamed and punished for someone else's mistakes.

WHIRL

— **give (something) a whirl** to give something a try to see if one likes it, finds it suitable, etc..

WHISKER
— **win by a whisker** to win by a very short amount.

WHISTLE
— **wet one's whistle** to have a drink.
— **whistle for (something)** to ask for (something) with no hope of getting it.

WHITE
— **a whited sepulchre** someone who pretends to be moral and virtuous but is in fact bad.
— **white lie** a not very serious lie.
— **whiter than white** extremely honest and moral.

WHOOP
— **whoop it up** to celebrate in a noisy, extravagant way.

WICK
— **get on (someone's) wick** to annoy or irritate (someone) greatly.

WIDE
— **be wide open** used of a competition of some kind to indicate that it is very difficult to predict the winner as the competitors seem equally good.

WILD
— **a wild goose chase** a search or hunt that cannot end in success.
— **run wild** to behave in an uncontrolled, undisciplined way.
— **sow one's wild oats** to enjoy oneself in a wild and sometimes promiscuous way when one is young.
— **spread like wildfire** to spread extremely rapidly.

WILL
— **where there's a will there's a way**
— **with a will** enthusiastically and energetically.

WIND
— **get one's second wind** to find renewed energy to go on doing something after a period of feeling tired

and weak.

— **get wind of (something)** to receive information about (something) *indirectly or secretly.*

— **in the wind** about to happen, being placed or prepared.

— **get the wind up** to become frightened or nervous.

— **raise the wind** to get enough money to do (something).

— **spit in the wind** to try to do something impossible and so waste time and effort.

— **take the wind out of (someone's) sails** to reduce (someone's) pride in his or her cleverness, abilities, etc.

— **throw caution to the (four) winds** to begin to behave recklessly.

— **whistle in the wind** to make a statement or promise which is pointless since it is very unlikely to have any effect or produce any results.

WINDMILL

— **tilt at windmills** to struggle against imaginary opposition.

WINDOW

— **go out the window** to disappear completely; to be ignore or forgotten about.

— **window-dressing** the presentation of something to show the most favourable parts and hide the rest.

WING

— **on a wing and a prayer** used to indicate that you hope to do something successfully even although you do not have the resources to do so.

— **spread one's wings** (1) to leave home.

(2) to try to put into practice one's own ideas, to make use of one's abilities.

— **take (someone) under one's wing** to take (someone) under one's protection and guidance.

— **try one's wings** to try to do something which one has never done before in order to see if one will be successful at it.

— **waiting in the wings** in a state of readiness to do something, especially to take over someone else's job.
— **wing it** to do something without planning or preparation, to improvise.

WINK
— **not sleep a wink** not to be able to sleep at all.
— **tip (someone) the wink** to give (someone) information secretly or privately.

WIRE
— **down to the wire:** to the last possible minute.
— **get** *or* **have one's wires crossed** to be involved in a misunderstanding.
— **get in under the wire** to do something or get somewhere at the last possible minute.

WISE
— **a wise guy** someone who thinks that he is smart, knowledgeable, etc, and acts as if he is.
— **none the wiser** knowing no more than one did before.
— **put (someone) wise to (something)** to give (someone) information about (something), make (someone) aware of (something).

WISH
— **wishful thinking** believing that, or hoping that, something unlikely is true or will happen just because one wishes that it would.
— **wish (someone) joy of (something)** to wish that (something) will be a pleasure or benefit to someone (although one doesn't think it will).

WIT
— **at one's wits' end** worried and desperate.
— **keep one's wits about one** to be alert and watchful.
— **live by one's wits** to live by cunning schemes rather than by working.
— **pit one's wits against (someone)** to use one's intelligence to try to defeat (someone).

— **scare (someone) out of his** *or* **her wits** to frighten (someone) very much.

WITCH

— **witch-hunt** a search for and persecution of people who are thought to have done something wrong, hold opinions which are thought to be dangerous etc.

WOLF

— **a wolf in sheep's clothing** someone evil and dangerous who seems to be gentle and harmless.
— **cry wolf** to give a false warning of danger, to call unnecessarily for help.
— **keep the wolf from the door** to prevent poverty and hunger.

WONDER

— **no wonder** it is not surprising.

WOOD

— **not to be able to see the wood for the trees** not to be able to consider the general nature of a situation, etc, because one is concentrating too much on details.
— **out of the woods** out of danger or difficulties.
— **touch wood** to touch something made of wood supposedly to keep away bad luck.

WOODWORK

— **come out of the woodwork** suddenly to appear in large numbers.

WOOL

— **pull the wool over (someone's) eyes** to deceive (someone).
— **wool-gathering** day-dreaming.

WORD

— **eat one's words** to admit that one was wrong in what one said.
— **get a word in edgeways** *or* **edgewise** to have difficulty in breaking into a conversation.

— **hang on (someone's) words** to listen carefully and eagerly to everything that someone says.
— **have a word in (someone's) ear** to tell (someone) something in private.
— **have a word with (someone)** to have a short conversation with (someone).
— **have words** to argue or quarrel.
— **in a word** briefly.
— **keep one's word** to do as one promised to do.
— **put in a good word for (someone)** to say something favourable about (someone), to recommend (someone).
— **put words into (someone's) mouth** to say that someone has said something when he/she did not; to suggest that someone is going to say something when he/she has no intention of doing so.
— **say the word** say what you want and your wishes will be carried out.
— **take (someone) at his** *or* **her word** to believe (someone) without question and act accordingly.
— **take (someone's) word for it** to believe what someone says without question and without proof.
— **take the words out of (someone's) mouth** to say what (someone) was just about to say.
— **words fail me** I cannot put my feelings into words.

WORK
— **all work and no play makes Jack a dull boy** people should take some leisure time and not work all the time.
— give **(someone) the works** to give (someone) the complete treatment.
— **have one's work cut out** to face a very difficult task.
— **worked up** agitated, annoyed.
— **work out** to come to a successful conclusion.

WORLD
— **a man of the world** a sophisticated and worldly man.
— **come down in the world** to be less well off, less successful etc. than formerly.

— **come up in the world** to be better off, more successful, etc. than formerly.
— **do (someone) the world of good** to have a very good effect on (someone); to be of great benefit or advantage to (someone).
— **for all the world like (someone *or* something)** exactly like (someone or something).
— **not the end of the world** used to make someone realize that things are not as bad as they think they are.
— **not to have long for this world** to be about to die.
— **on top of the world** very cheerful and happy.
— **out of this world** remarkably good.
— **think the world of (someone)** to be extremely fond of (someone).
— **the world is (someone's) oyster** (someone) has a great many possible opportunities or chances.

WORM
— **a can of worms** an extremely complicated and difficult situation.
— **(even) the worm turns** even the most humble or meek person will protest if treated badly enough.

WORSE
— **be none the worse for (something)** not to have been harmed or badly affected by (something).

WORTH
— **for all one is worth** using maximum effort.

WOUND
— **lick one's wounds** to try to recover from a situation in which one has been badly defeated or humiliated.
— **reopen old wounds** to remind people of past unpleasant experiences which they would prefer to forget about.

WRAP
— **keep (something) under wraps** to keep (something) secret or hidden.

— **take the wraps off (something)** to reveal, or give details about, something that has been secret up till now.
— **wrapped up in (someone *or* something)** absorbed in, giving all one's attention to (someone or something).
— **wrap (something) up** to finish (something) completely.

WRINGER
— **be put through the wringer** to have experienced a very difficult or painful period or situation.

WRIT
— **writ large** used to indicate that something is in its most extreme form.

WRITE
— **the writing on the wall** something which indicates that something unpleasant, such as failure, unhappiness, disaster, etc, will happen.

WRONG
— **be in the wrong** to be blameworthy, to be guilty of error.
— **get on the wrong side of (someone)** to cause (someone) to dislike or be hostile to one.
— **not to put a foot wrong** not to make a mistake of any kind.

# Y

YARN

— **spin a yarn** to tell a long story, especially an untrue one that is given as an excuse.

YEAR

— **the** year **dot** a long time, the beginning of time.

YESTERDAY

— **not born yesterday** experienced and not easily fooled.

YOUNG

— **you're only young once** one should take advantage of the opportunities that arise when one is young and has the energy, freedom, etc, to enjoy or exploit them.

# Z

ZERO

— **zero hour** the time at which something is due to begin.

— **zero in** to reach a conclusion.